IMMORTAL

IMMORTAL

ERICA BARNES

www.urbanbooks.net

Urban Books, LLC
1199 Straight Path
West Babylon, NY 11704

Immortal copyright © 2009 Erica Barnes

ISBN- 13: 978-1-60162-170-2
ISBN- 10: 1-60162-170-1

First Printing November 2009
Printed in the United States of America

10 9 8 7 6 5 4 3 2 1

This is a work of fiction. Any references or similarities to actual events, real people, living, or dead, or to real locales are intended to give the novel a sense of reality. Any similarity in other names, characters, places, and incidents is entirely coincidental.

Distributed by Kensington Publishing Corp.
Submit Wholesale Orders to:
Kensington Publishing Corp.
C/O Penguin Group (USA) Inc.
Attention: Order Processing
405 Murray Hill Parkway
East Rutherford, NJ 07073-2316
Phone: 1-800-526-0275
Fax: 1-800-227-9604

IMMORTAL

Prologue

"Hurry up, man!" I yelled to Aaron who was lagging behind the rest of the group. "Let's go, man! C'mon!" I got behind him and pushed him forward. I made a mental note to never rob a liquor store with a dude who was overweight and out of shape. Pablo and Rock were almost around the corner and here I was pushing Aaron's big ass to cover. The robbery was supposed to be quick, but Aaron slowed us down. Pablo, Rock, and I could hold our own, but we would never leave our fellow friend behind.

Pablo, Rock, and Aaron were my homeboys from Van Ness Gangsters. Pablo was the toughest of us all. His "don't give a fuck" mentality was inherited from growing up in the tough streets of South Central. Bounced around from foster home to foster home, Pablo found comfort in the gangs. He wanted a sense of belonging and found that in gangsters who were always looking to recruit. Because Pablo was a hard-ass and knew how to fight for his, he wore his gang on his sleeve. He made a reputation for himself the moment he got into Van Ness Gangsters and immediately climbed his way to the top. Rock was Pablo's best friend and was pressured into joining the gang. Rock was always sheltered by his mother as a child and never had a sense of independence anyway. Pablo and five other gang members jumped Rock into the hood earlier this year. Aaron was a different story. In elementary, Aaron was the fat kid who always got bullied. All throughout middle school he was bullied and ridiculed about his weight. Once in high school, Van Ness Gangsters had its newest member. The need for respect was so strong he was willing to become a gangster to get it.

Me, I'm a different story. Growing up, gangs were all I knew. My grandfather was a radical Black Panther who went corrupt, my daddy was one of the original bloods to exist in Los Angeles, and my mother was a gangbanger as well. I lived and breathed gangs. I lost my dad to gang violence and I lost my mother to crack when I was younger. I grew up with my uncle, who was a gangster and pimp, and his ho of a wife. I was alone and had to raise myself, just like most of the young kids I knew had to. The streets were calling. I answered their call and became a blood at age thirteen. For the past four years I've been going hard.

Pablo, Rock, Aaron, and I had just robbed Old Jessie's liquor store strapped with heat and beanies over our faces with the eyes cut out. As the braver than any other, Pablo held Jessie at gunpoint and cursed him out something vicious, Rock stood as a watch out while I ransacked the cash register for money. I grabbed the lockbox that I knew held some more cash. Aaron's hungry ass had already dug into a honey bun while we were robbing the store.

The whole thing took less than five minutes. We were in and out of there in a flash. Now we were running underneath the streetlights on the streets of Los Angeles, some lights on, some flickering and the others broken. The evening sky was our only ally, helping us blend in with the shadows of the night. Our destination, Fifty-fourth street, was three blocks away. We got to Fifty-fourth street and it seemed empty, deprived of life as we dashed for cover. The police wouldn't take long to get to the scene, being that they were right up the way. Aaron was deadweight and a whole lot of it. I had every right in my mind to leave him here to get caught but I would never leave the homie hanging, no matter how big he was. Besides, I wasn't sure if Aaron would snitch if he was asked to tell on his boys anyway. I was going to push Aaron to the destination.

I looked down the street and saw that Pablo and Rock were gone. They must've made it to my god-sister Danielle's house already. Aaron fell to the ground and started wheezing uncontrollably. I thought he was having a heart attack, and then realized it was an asthma attack.

"Where the fuck is your inhaler, Aaron?" I yelled at him. I kneeled down and tried to help him off the ground.

"I think—it—fell," he wheezed.

"Where?" I asked. "In the store or on the street?"

"On the street," he breathed.

"Try to crawl down the street or something," I told him, frustrated. "I'm going to get it." I ran down the street hoping to get the inhaler before the police started circling the area. If they found Aaron's inhaler with his name plastered all over it, they could use that as evidence and it would lead to Aaron, leading to us.

Pissed off, I sped up the pace as I heard the police sirens getting louder. I ran and searched for the inhaler on the ground. An extra thirty seconds can mean a whole lot. I did not see the inhaler on the ground and that only pissed me off even more. Now my conscience was telling me to forget the inhaler. I ran onto Arlington, which was a shortcut to Danielle's house. Heading down the street toward me was a police car. I changed directions and ran back the opposite way. In my view was another police car heading toward the liquor store.

Damn, police already on my ass, I thought. *I hope Aaron is okay.* Police were hot on my trail. I was on foot, they were in cars. What the hell was I thinking? My chances of getting away were slim to none. Why was I wasting my time running?

"Put your hands up behind your head!" the policemen yelled in unison after they cornered me in a driveway.

I did as I was told and let two of the officers come and check me for any weapons. They found the stolen money in my pockets. They slung me to the concrete and put the handcuffs on my wrists. They roughly pulled me off the ground and escorted me to the back of the police car.

I was going to jail for the third time, and I was only seventeen.

Chapter One

Welcome Home

"One . . . Two . . . Three! "Surprise!"
I was greeted by my closest friends and relatives. I was glad to be back home, where I belonged. I had no desire of going back to jail. It had been three long years since I had seen the streets of California. Now that I was back, I was going to live it up, but not too much. I had to do my best to stay out of jail—it's no place to be. I received warm hugs and manly handshakes. All these people were here to celebrate my comeback.

While I was incarcerated, Moseley, my little homie, stayed by my side. He and I spoke every day, keeping me updated on what was going on while I was locked up. Moseley and I went to Fairfax High School together. I was older than Moseley by one year. I was the gangbanger while he was the kid who wanted to get put on but was not sure. Moseley started going to church on Sunday mornings, Sunday nights, and Wednesday evenings for Bible study, and Friday nights for youth service. Me? Let's just say I wasn't the most religious man in the world. Seeing Moseley today struck interest in me. Something had changed about him and I hoped to find out what it was by the end of the day.

Calvin, my homeboy was a coldhearted, trash-talking, hard-ass that lived by his own rules and broke them as well. He lived by the words of Tupac and actually got the words *Me Against The World* tattooed on his back. But what could I expect from somebody whose role model is Suge Knight? Although he was in a gang, Calvin was a low-profile gang member. He put in work for his hood, but didn't have to put his gangbanging business out in the open. He was well-known for his fighting skills. A nigga could throw down! Pulling him away from a fight was damn near impossible unless you wanted to get harmed yourself. In his mind, Calvin wanted to end the fight standing over the knocked-out, cold body of his opponent. And each time, that's what he did. Calvin was determined to prove to others he was tough, and didn't have to wear his gang on his sleeve to be that way.

Anthony, however, was the exact opposite of me, Moseley, and Calvin. The multitalented young man was a star all around. He excelled in school, worked a legal job, dressed so fly it was ridiculous, and could dance and sing. He was a ladies' man to the fullest. Why he chose to hang out with people like Calvin, Moseley, and me remains a mystery.

I shook my boys' hand and told them how great it felt to be back. Moseley poured me a cup of straight Hennessy and Calvin handed me a blunt to go with it.

"Nah, man, I can't even do that. You know my parole officer makes me take a drug test. I got to be clean," I said, refusing the party favors.

"Nigga fuck that!" Calvin said. "You can fuck with that water pill and clean out your system."

I shook my head and answered, "Nope, I don't even want to go that route. But I'm still gon'' party!" I was determined to enjoy my homecoming celebration without the weed and liquor.

Moseley, Anthony, Calvin, and I went around the living room greeting the guests like celebrities. There was one guest that I did not have to greet. I just looked at her and she already knew everything was good.

Her name was Shay Dawes. Before I got locked up for three years, Shay and I use to talk. It was nothing serious because she wasn't trying to be with a gangbanger. At the time, I just wanted to make her my girl because she was just that sexy. With pussy being thrown at me from different directions, Shay was always skeptical. I never got the chance to take her down, proving she was special and wasn't giving it up without a fight. Shay and I never had sex, but I damn sure wanted to when I saw how good she looked.

Her long and thick brown hair reached the middle of her back. She was five feet four and blessed with a figure, thick—just the way I liked it. Her eyes were light brown and seemed to penetrate me whenever I looked into them. Shay had what I call a sophisticated ghetto talk. She spoke clearly and wasn't illiterate, but she had the ghetto girl accent and I loved it. It goes to show that sometimes the girl doesn't live in the ghetto, the ghetto lives in the girl.

"Hey Khalid," she said. Hearing her say my name made me feel warm inside.

I approached her and embraced her in a passionate hug, lifting her up off the floor. She giggled and demanded that I put her down. I put her down and kissed her cheek as I ran my hands down her back. "I missed you the most," I said.

"Yeah right," said the skeptical Shay I knew from way back then. "I'm going to pray you stay out of jail for at least the next three years."

I shook my head and said, "You don't have to worry about that because Khalid is here to stay!"

"That's what you said last time," Shay said with an ambiguous look.

"Well, thank God for second chances, right?" Dior, asked cutting into the conversation. She stepped around Shay and gave me a hug after receiving a look of approval from Calvin.

Dior was Calvin's girlfriend of four years. They had some major ups and downs, but both were determined to make the relationship work. There were times where the only moments they got along were in bed, and there were also times when the two were inseparable. Dior did not want to belong to anyone else and Calvin sure did not want her to.

Dior was a sassy, stubborn, and devoted to love. She stood five feet five with a nice figure that Calvin could not get enough of. Her skin was a fair caramel brown and her hair was dyed reddish brown. She was journalism major at Cal State San Bernardino and in her spare time a materialistic princess with the fear of going broke. But as long as Calvin kept her pockets full, she would not have that fear. She worked as an intern at a local magazine company and hoped she would be offered a job there when her internship was over.

Dior was crazy in love with Calvin. She referred to their relationship as the "designer couple" (Christian *Dior* and *Calvin* Klein). Dior brought out the lighter side of Calvin, but if she fucked up, she was bound to catch his bad alter ego.

"Hey Dior, I guess I missed you a little bit," I laughed.

She lightly punched me in my arm. "Shut up, Khalid! I hope you enjoy this party because I helped with the decorations."

I nodded my head. "Yeah, they're okay. Next time, don't reuse decorations from the previous party," I joked.

Dior shook her head and laughed. "Glad you're back,"

she said smiling. Calvin grabbed her hand and brought her into his arms.

I called for Danielle. She came out from the kitchen and asked me what it was that I needed. I told her to put on some music so we could really turn this homecoming into a party. Once the music came on, the guests loosened up.

Dior was already dancing with Calvin. Moseley was bobbing his head as we partied the hood way. Anthony was entertaining everybody as he jokingly did old-school dances in the middle of the room.

A joyous feeling came over me. I had never felt so exuberant in my life. The last two times I came home from being locked up, I went right back to gangbanging. There was no celebration, there was no party. It was simply about what I was going to do for the hood next. This time, I was going to make every effort to stay out of jail. Not only for myself, but for my friends that wanted me to stay around.

I looked around at everyone enjoying themselves. When my eyes reached the door, I saw Pablo, Rock, and Aaron. These were my thug homies, my fellow gangbangers. Pablo and Rock didn't get caught and Aaron's ass managed to hide in a junky backyard, where he later found his asthma inhaler in his back pocket. When the detectives asked me to come clean on whom I was with, I didn't. Even when they offered to reduce my sentence, I still declined. So even though we all did the crime, I was the only one who did the time. At that age, I was more concerned with keeping my street credit as a gangsta. I wouldn't want to come home with the newfound reputation of a snitch. Even at age twenty, I wouldn't have snitched. Something inside me just disagrees with selling your boys out because you got busted.

I walked over to them and greeted them with the blood handshake. They didn't look too glad to see me. I was surprised because these were my boys who should be glad I was home.

I asked, "So what the fuck? Y'all niggas lookin' like you wanted me to stay in jail."

"What up, Khalid?" Pablo asked solemnly with a nod of his head.

I looked at him like he had three heads instead of one. Pablo never called me by my real name, Khalid. He always called me by my given hood name, Hide. It came as a nickname from my uncle because whenever he threatened to beat me I would hide so good that he couldn't find me. That evolved into my hood name for Van Ness Gangsters. I wanted to be so damn gangsta that whenever I came around my enemies would duck and hide.

"Y'all ain't hit a nigga up in jail. I don't know what the fuck is going on. Where y'all been?"

"Here," Rock answered. "In the city."

"Yeah, I know. I tried to call y'all couple of times but you wasn't ever available . . . all of a sudden," I said. I was now giving them intimidating looks while getting similar looks of my own.

"We were still tryna take care of business. Shit went down while you were locked up," Pablo answered, not looking me in the face. Instead, he was looking around the room.

"Well, remember that I'm the reason y'all niggas were still doing your thing," I reminded them. "I had y'all back. The least y'all coulda did was seen ya nigga who was locked up! It's been three fucking years and I don't know who the fuck y'all are."

Aaron cleared his throat and said, "Yo Khalid, calm down, man!"

"Fuck that, homie!" I exclaimed. I don't know what got into me, but I was starting to lose my cool. "Nigga, you the reason why I got locked up. I went back to get your inhaler and you had the shit all along, blood! Shoulda left your fat ass in the street!"

Aaron looked me up and down. "I told you to calm down. The reason why yo ass got caught was 'cuz you was slow on your feet!"

"The fuck you talkin' 'bout? Slow on my feet? Nigga, you the fat ass who fell out!" I yelled. By this time the music had stopped and people were looking in our direction.

Moseley, Calvin, and Anthony had begun making their way toward me and the niggas I was looking at in a whole new light. Pablo had balled his fists up as if he was going to swing on me any moment now.

"Y'all some fake-ass niggas, blood!" I spat. "Couldn't even answer a call or see a nigga in jail and got the nerve to show up to this party."

"Nigga, fuck you! I ain't gotta do a dance 'cuz your ass is back! Ain't like I wanted you in jail. I suggest you stop talkin' out the ass!" Rock yelled.

"Watch how you talking to the homie, blood!" Calvin said.

"On 20s bloods y'all niggas is trippin!" Moseley said.

"Fuck 20s," Pablo spat.

This is how gangs started beefing with gangs that wear the same color. Somebody disses another hood (of the same color), they take offense, and beat some ass. Word spreads and we got intergang warfare going down. Set trippin', straight up.

"Fuck what, blood?" Calvin said. He wanted to say some words back, but not being one for words, took it into action. Calvin swung on Pablo, and that began the brutal fight between two sets of my friends. But after Rock suckerpunched me in my jaw, I knew who my boys were and who wasn't. It was Moseley, Calvin, Anthony, and me against Pablo, Rock, and Aaron.

Calvin and Pablo were going at it like two vicious pit bulls trying to kill each other. There was blood running from Pablo's nose and Calvin was now sporting a busted lip. I think Pablo had found his match and didn't want to lose. Moseley surprised the hell out of me as he stood his ground with Rock. Even though he was a mere five feet six inches, Moseley boxed the hell out of Rock who was an even six feet. It took both me and Anthony to knock Aaron's big ass down. Aaron had grabbed Anthony by the neck and attempted to choke slam his ass to the floor. I came behind and punched Aaron in his side. He dropped Anthony and turned around to face me and I quickly jabbed him in his eye.

"Move! Move out of the way!" Dior said, pushing the crowd to get to the front of the circle surrounding us. She easily spotted her boyfriend Calvin in a bloody fight. "Calvin, stop! Stop it, baby!" she screamed as if he was beating her.

When some older men found the strength to break up the fights, Dior went over to Calvin and tried to calm him down.

"Fuck yo' hood, nigga!" he rampaged. He sent deadly looks toward Pablo, who was being held back.

Pablo shook loose and charged toward Calvin, not even caring that Dior was nearby. Pablo grabbed Dior by the shoulders and abruptly pushed her into the wall, the dumbest thing he could have done. Nobody put their hands on Calvin's girl. Calvin and Pablo threw violent punches at each other, causing each of their boys to pull them apart.

"Leave the fucking party!" Danielle told Pablo, Rock, and Aaron. "Get out now!"

Pablo, Rock, and Aaron left the party through the front door after making it clear that the beef was not over. Danielle insisted that the doors be locked just in case they tried to come back. She turned up the music, hoping people didn't lose their partying mood.

"Damn, blood," Moseley said to me. "I thought y'all was cool!"

I shook my head. "Fuck those fake-ass niggas," I replied. I looked at Moseley, who had a couple of scratches on his face. Other than the scratches, he was quite all right. I turned to Anthony, who was clean as a whistle. That was probably because I did all the work. Calvin, on the other hand, came out with a busted lip, which was probably because he was in the bloodiest fight. I would've helped him out but I knew Calvin could handle his own weight. Anthony would've been murdered by Aaron if I didn't assist him.

Dior took Calvin to the kitchen and sat him down in a chair. She retrieved some ice out of the freezer and placed it in a plastic bag. She wrapped a paper towel around the plastic bag and told Calvin to hold it on his lip. She got a rag and ran it under warm water.

"I hate when you fight, Calvin!" she said as she stood over him and wiped away the blood from his lip.

"Well, he disrespected Khalid," Calvin said.

"Then Khalid shoulda handled that," Dior replied.

"And he disrespected the hood," Calvin said, insisting the fight was well worth it.

Dior sucked her teeth and said, "It wasn't your fight to begin with." She held the warm rag over his mouth so he could not speak. Like a mother to a child, she cleaned his bloody mouth and aided his bruises. She held his face in her hand and said, "Stop fighting. Okay?" Calvin nodded. She kissed his lips, busted and all.

"Sorry about all that, Dior. Y'all okay?" I asked.

"You don't have to apologize to me, Khalid. I can't believe they even showed up. I'm just glad everyone's okay," Dior replied.

Calvin and Dior returned to the party after I made sure everything was all good between them. I searched the room for Shay, talking among her friends near the hallway of the house. I made my way over to her and tapped her on the shoulder. I summoned her into a corner.

"Sorry about that, Shay, but where were we before all these interruptions?" I asked as I twirled the ends of her hair in my fingers.

She shook her head sassily and rolled her eyes. She said, "Damn, Khalid. You still at it, ain't you? Did you not learn anything from jail?"

Yeah, I thought, *that I don't wanna go back*. "I know you ain't referring to the fight. Calvin was fighting more than I was."

"This isn't about Calvin, Khalid. It's about you," Shay replied. "Some old habits never die, huh?"

I took her hand in mine. "You gon' dance or not? A nigga just got out of jail and can't get a dance?"

"Like that's what he really wants," Shay answered.

Shay was putting on a front. It was as if she couldn't even open up to me anymore. Before I went to jail Shay was more accepting and playful. Now she was on some play-hard-to-get shit that I personally didn't give a damn for. There were only three reasons I narrowed down to, as to why Shay had a change in personality. One was she had heard some nasty rumors about me, something a jealous ex-girlfriend constructed or, two, I "dropped the soap" while locked up. And three, she had a new man. Hell, it could've been a combination. At the moment, I wasn't going to try to figure out something that I knew would come out soon. I just led Shay to the middle of the room and we danced. We danced, hoping to gain the friendship we had three years ago.

I've been known to have a keen eye . . . especially for detail. I noticed the differences in all of my friends, except

Anthony. He would stay the same old, goofy boy I met in school. But take Moseley, for example. Three years ago he was a timid and shy guy who stayed in the background. Now he was trying to be respected and strong. He talked and walked differently. I saw the new man he was in his behavior. Moseley was on a whole new game. Calvin, on the other hand, kept his thug edge. However, after the fight, I knew it was wearing away slowly. The old Calvin would not have let anyone pull him away from Pablo. Calvin would've murdered him with bare hands. Even if I was right about the thug in Calvin turning soft, I would never be exactly sure. Calvin would fight it to the death. He would never want to be seen as soft, let alone easy going in a fight.

Dior was more passionate nowadays, unlike her boyfriend. I was used to Dior being less reasonable and having a lot of attitude. Some of her sassiness had disappeared. From her actions toward Calvin—even by the way they were dancing—Dior was different. She seemed clingier and more dependent on Calvin.

Now I could've been exactly right or awfully wrong in the observation of my friends, but something had changed over the last three years . . . something. It was going to drive me crazy on the inside until I found out. Another thing I did want to know was if my friends would see the change in me. Moreover, would they be a part of the change I was trying to make in my life?

Only time would tell.

Chapter Two

Moseley

Shortly after I moved in with my boys, I picked up on the routine. Moseley was definitely the butler of the house. He cooked, cleaned, and kept the house in pretty good condition whenever Dior wasn't over playing mom. He was responsible for the majority of the rent. Whereas Calvin and Anthony took care of the utilities and the leftover three hundred dollars on the rent. Calvin ran up the water bill like crazy by taking hour-long showers. Anthony was not always responsible for groceries, but he sure as hell ate through the fridge and cabinets. If it wasn't Anthony buying food, Dior was sure to come by with groceries to stock up the kitchen. She played a major role in how well kept the house was. All it took was a call from Calvin saying, "Come over here and clean up." Dior would be there in a flash wearing some sweats, old tennis shoes, and a tank top.

I felt sorry that Dior was the maid for these guys. Any opportunity I had to clean up, I took. After a month of me living there, Dior found herself rarely coming over to clean—only to see Calvin for some dick or a date.

Moseley and I were chilling in the living room. He was drinking a cup of E&J, watching music videos. What better time to ask Moseley about his new attitude than now.

"Damn, it's been a minute since we was able to chill, huh? What you been doing while a nigga got locked up?" I asked him.

Moseley paused to sip from the cup. "Man, just been out here banging for the hood blood!" he answered.

Hood? Blood? Banging? Moseley seemed to have gotten gangsta overnight. "What hood, Moseley? I know you don't bang."

"Hell yeah, blood!" Moseley said, standing up. He took the shirt off his back so I could see the giant tattoo of Twenty-fourth street on his back.

"You got put on 20s, Moseley?" I asked somewhat proud and otherwise shocked.

"Yup, right at the park. Ask Calvin, he was one of the niggas who jumped me in," he replied.

"How many of them was it?" I asked.

"Shit, like fifteen," Moseley answered. He kept his shirt off and sat back down.

I shook my head. "I would've never expected you to get put on a hood."

"Why not? 'cuz y'all niggas used to think I was a bitch, huh?" Moseley asked. "Fuck y'all! Everybody knows Mo goes hard now!"

"Mo? That's a new nickname or something? Is it short for Moseley?" I asked jokingly.

"Yeah, and it means the mo' money I get the mo' problems," Moseley said, expecting an approval or a laugh.

I guess he was trying to sound cool, but he would always be little Moseley to me. "Moseley, you were like the one friend I never expected to get put on a hood. Why you fuck up and do some shit like that?"

"Why is it considered 'fucking up' when I get put on? Calvin got put on. You got put on. It's considered G when y'all do it," Moseley defended.

"Trust me, if I could take back getting put on a gang, I would. And as far as Calvin goes, he's crazy, so enough said. But I always thought you'd stay away from that shit and become successful," I said.

Moseley sucked his teeth and said, "Nigga, thugs can become successful too. Look at Tupac."

"Dead," I said.

"Eazy-E."

"Dead."

"The Game."

"Can you name a successful person from the hood that isn't in the music industry? How many niggas from round our way actually make it to that kind of status? None, right?" I stated.

"Well, then, you become successful, blood," Moseley said.

"Success ain't made for everybody," I said. "Believe me. It's not that I don't want to be, I just don't know if I'm cut out for it. All the shit I've been through? Success seems like a joke. I only have one goal. Stay the fuck out of trouble." There was an awkward pause. I continued, "So you been wildin' out with 20s?"

Moseley answered, "On King Day at the parade. We got into it with some 30s. Man, that shit was fuckin' crazy as hell, blood."

I nodded my head. I had a hard time painting the image of Moseley throwing down on the 30s crips in the middle of Martin Luther King Boulevard. But if he said it happened, I had no other choice but to believe him until proven otherwise. My thoughts were obviously written all over my face.

"What's wrong with you, blood? You thought I couldn't

be on a gang? Damn, you underestimated a nigga too?"
Moseley asked, kicking his feet up on the table in front of
him.

I shrugged my shoulders. "I didn't say I underestimated
you, I just never pictured you in a gang. Understand that,
my nigga. Out of all of us you was the good one."

"Nah, homie, I was the bitch! Now that I got a little
street credit, people finding it hard to believe," Moseley
said.

"Why you getting so offended, man? Do you, my nigga!
I never said you were bitch, and I ain't trippin' on you.
That's what you wanted to do, so do it!" I blurted out. I
was fed up with how hard Moseley was acting. There was
no need for him to backfire at everything I said. If Moseley
was banging like he claimed to be, then his actions would
clearly speak for themselves. "Who you know from the
hood?"

"Big homie Nite, Jordan, Slim . . . uh, the big homie
Kush." Moseley stopped. He felt he named big names from
20s.

I knew every last one of them. I knew it was fact. Moseley or Mo, was a 20s blood.

Chapter Three

Calvin

Over the weeks, I grew accustomed to who did what and who acted like what in the house. Moseley was the little man, proving he may be a thorough gangbanger, but to his boys he was still the punk. Anthony was back and forth between school and work. He was rarely found at home except on late nights and some weekends. He would spend the night at one of his girls' house if it got too late.

Calvin was the homebody. Of course, he had his reasons for staying home and that came into play when Dior came over. Sometimes she would stay for three nights at a time. She and Calvin would stay cooped up in his room, watching movies or making love. Calvin only left the house for work or if somebody made him mad. If that was the case, he'd stay with his cousin Evan.

Moseley, Anthony, and I just tried to stay out of Calvin's way. We were more than happy when Dior came over. They would stay in his room for hours at a time. We knew what was going down . . . and gave Calvin his props for having a girl who would give him pussy any time of day or night.

It was just like any other Friday when Dior came through.

She had a wide smile on her face as I opened the front door. I knew the smile was because Calvin was off of work and she was going to get some sexual healing.

"Hey, Khalid!" she said cheerfully. "Is my boo home?"

I nodded. "Yeah, he in his room. Come on in," I said, inviting her inside.

With her D&G sunglasses on and a Betsey Johnson purse, Dior strolled into the house. "Who's all here?" she asked, pulling her shades above her hairline.

"Just me and your boy," I answered as I followed her to Calvin's room.

Dior nodded and walked down the hall toward Calvin's room. She entered the bedroom and found Calvin watching ESPN on his 32-inch television. The television was on mute and the stereo was on full blast, blazing Tupac's "Ambitionz Az A Ridah." Dior sat down on the bed with him and took a drink from his cup of Jose Cuervo and Kool-Aid. She gulped down the drink and looked at him. Calvin was already drunk and Dior wasted no time in getting tipsy herself.

"How long have you been drinking today?" she asked, taking more Jose Cuervo and adding it to the concoction.

"For like twenty minutes," Calvin said. His hand moved toward Dior's waist. He ran his fingertips along her sides.

"Stop, babe! That tickles!" Dior giggled. I left the room at this point because I know what was coming next.

I walked by the bedroom and overhead part of the conversation.

"Call for Daddy," Calvin commanded.

"Oooh, Daddy!" Dior moaned.

"Louder, baby!"

"*Ah Daddy!*"

"Who Daddy?"

"Ah, you Daddy!"

"Who?"

"Calvin!"

Damn, Calvin got it like that, I thought as I snickered to myself. I heard a couple of smacks that I figured went to Dior's backside. I heard a couple of more *Daddys* followed by a loud, long moan. Dior must've reached her peak. Then, footsteps made their way to the door and I couldn't get away fast enough. Calvin caught me in the middle of running for cover.

I looked at him and gave him a sarcastic thumbs up. Calvin chuckled and nodded. "Nigga like that?" I said.

"Hell yeah," Calvin said, going into the bathroom.

I snuck a look into the bedroom and saw Dior laid out on the bed with the sheets covering only her ass. I smiled to myself and proceeded into the kitchen. I began fixing myself a sandwich and no less than five minutes later I was greeted by Calvin. He sat down in a chair at the kitchen table.

"I know you miss getting pussy," Calvin joked as he took a cigarette out of the carton and placed the carton on the table. "You ain't had none in a minute, man."

I wasn't amused at Calvin, obviously trying to be funny. I gave him a disapproving look and said, "Yeah, you right. I ain't had none in a minute. But that's all good because I'm want to hit this chick tonight."

"Who? Shay?" Calvin asked.

"I wish, blood," I admitted. "It's this girl I met down the street. Her name is Ebony."

Calvin looked at me with raised eyebrows. "Ebony? Ebony Coleman?"

I shrugged. "I don't know her last name," I answered.

"Okay," Calvin said. "She's brown-skinned?"

"Yup, with green eyes?"

"Those are contacts, blood," Calvin informed.

"Whatever," I said. "She got braids in her hair, and she not too thick, but she got a lil' something."

Calvin nodded. "Yeah, I know her. I messed with her too."

"You fucked her?" I asked.

Calvin put his finger up to his lips. "Don't let my girl hear you. Nah, I ain't fuck that girl. She was only good enough to suck my dick."

"How long ago was this?" I asked, feeling relieved about not talking to a girl who had slept with my homeboy.

"Last year," Calvin answered. "And yes, I was still with Dior."

I shook my head. "Do you still cheat on her?" I asked, knowing Calvin was one to get at another female every blue moon.

"Nah, that was old Calvin. This Calvin is a new man," he replied after taking a hit of his Newport cigarette.

"Why the change?" I asked.

Calvin shrugged his shoulders and shook his head. "Man, I can't really say. It was like this—" he hesitated. "I was in an argument with her about a number she found in my phone. I wanted to know why the hell she was in a nigga phone anyway, but she was too pissed off to answer that question. Then she started saying shit like how she really loved me and needed me. She was all disappointed in a nigga 'cuz I let her down. She was saying how she would do anything for me and just wanted to know the truth. I swear on my life, Khalid, after that day I knew I had a down-ass bitch on my team and I don't want to do shit to fuck it up."

"I know staying faithful can be hard as hell, huh?" I asked, taking a bite of my sandwich.

Calvin agreed and said, "Oh yeah, but when I come home to a female like Dior, that shit is simple."

There was an awkward pause. Dior called for Calvin. He stood up and said, "Yeah, blood. It's time for round number two!" He rubbed his hands together and went back into the room, but not before finishing off the last of the cigarette.

The music volume was turned up a couple notches, insuring that no one would hear them. Calvin and Dior's sex session made me want to get some pussy of my own. I only hoped I wouldn't get whipped like how Calvin seemed to be. I would've thought he would stay a player for life—no bullshitting. But I guess when you find the one, then she really is the only one.

Back in the day, Calvin was the man in high school by being one of the most sought-after guys there. Females plagued after Calvin, but only a selected few went far. Dior was the girl after Calvin's own heart, but back then he was less excited about it. Now he was on something new. He wanted Dior and Dior only. Neither one of them could picture the other being with someone else. I knew for damn sure Dior didn't want to belong to another guy and she definitely couldn't live with Calvin being with another girl.

Calvin was known to be selfish, demanding that Dior not talk to any other males. Dior hated the rule, being that she had heard rumors about Calvin messing around with other girls and later found out they were true. Calvin was a walking double standard by asking Dior to do right by him, but wronging their relationship by fooling with other girls. Still, Dior hung in there. All her hard work had certainly paid off because now she had Calvin in the position of faithfulness.

But as with any relationship, it wasn't perfect. They certainly had been in this position before, where everything is glittering but it still isn't gold.

Chapter Four

Anthony

The next afternoon, Anthony and I spent hours getting ready for a party we heard was being thrown in Inglewood. Ever since I met Anthony in high school, he was always the best dresser. He wasn't your typical hood star rocking Dickies pants, Chucks or a khaki suit. Anthony always dressed to impressed in top designers that had not made their way to the hood. He could be seen shopping at boutiques for men in Beverly Hills or Hollywood somewhere. His favorite streets, other than Crenshaw, were Sunset and Melrose. His footwear always matched his clothes. I could picture Anthony making it big in the fashion industry, and that is exactly what he wanted to do. He hoped to come out with his clothing line and be one of the few straight men with one.

Anthony stood in a slight lean with one arm folded across his chest and the other underneath his chin. He examined my outfit from the hat to the shos. "Hmm," he groaned.

I sucked my teeth angrily. "C'mon, man! You've been

looking at me for five minutes straight! What's wrong with my outfit, Anthony?"

Anthony shook his head. "Nothing, Khalid. I guess you look a'ight. Hopefully the lights will be off," he responded.

I retrieved my wallet from off of the dresser. "What is that suppose to mean?"

Anthony answered, "It's just if someone was to look at your outfit too long they'd get confused. You look good for the first five minutes."

"Whateva, nigga," I said, walking out the door.

"I was only joking, man," Anthony replied, putting his arm around my shoulder. "You look good, damn good. Hell, I helped you coordinate that outfit."

His sense of style did indeed help me look good. Doing it with ease, Anthony could point out a wardrobe malfunction and easily prescribe a remedy. He was one of the guys who dressed their asses off so you had to keep him in the crew. Being seen with Anthony made Moseley, Calvin, and me look stylish even if we were not as dressed up as he was.

Anthony and I walked into the living room where Moseley was waiting in plaid shorts, a bright yellow Ralph Lauren polo, and some colorful Nike dunks. Even I could agree my outfit was better than his. He jingled the keys to his car.

"Well, don't you look—" Anthony searched to find the words.—"colorful."

Calvin was on the sofa, dressed in basketball shorts, socks, and wife beater—a sign that he was obviously not going out with us.

"You sure you don't want to come?" I asked Calvin as I headed toward the door.

Calvin shook his head and kept his eyes glued on the television. "Nah, man. I'm good," he said.

"Damn, Calvin. I got out of jail and I haven't even

kicked it with all my boys at the same time. Just come with us," I insisted.

"Nigga, I said I'm good," Calvin snapped.

Any other day I would have snapped back, but I was in a cheery mood and I didn't want anything or anyone fucking it up.

"Well, fuck you too," I mumbled under my breath. Only Anthony heard me and in response he snickered as we walked out of the door.

The sun had just set and the stars were not even visible in the sky. I breathed in the night air as we headed toward Moseley's car. The temperature tonight was just right, about eighty-five degrees. Enjoying the Los Angeles weather was certainly something I missed doing while behind bars. I was going to take all the opportunities I had to appreciate the little things, weather included.

"Something is wrong with him," Anthony said. "Which one of us pissed him off this time?"

"Nah, it was probably Dior. She got that nigga going soft," Moseley said.

"Well, that's his issue. A nigga like me is ready to get his party on. What's good with the females, though?" I asked, quickly changing the subject.

"That's what I'm trying to find out," Anthony laughed. "Bet I pull the most ladies tonight. Matter of fact, Moseley, I'll pull one for you, okay?"

"Fuck you," Moseley laughed.

We got in the car and headed toward the party, a city over in Inglewood. Moseley turned up the volume on the radio and sped off into the street. Moseley took Adams to Crenshaw and took Crenshaw down to Stocker. By time we got on Stocker Street toward Inglewood, Moseley had got a call from his fling Natasha. She wanted him to come through and pick her up to go to the party.

"Fuck her," Anthony protested. "Going to Watts is sending us back. She should have called earlier."

"She heard you, Anthony! She said shut up," Moseley said. "Tasha, I'm going to call you back." Moseley got off the phone with her. "Well, peep this. I can drop you two off at the party, pick her up, and meet y'all back at the party."

I turned around and looked at Anthony in the backseat. He said, "Yeah right, Moseley. You pulled that routine when me, you, and Calvin went to Aisha's party. Let me tell you, Khalid. Natasha called when we were on our way to the party and she said she wanted to come. Moseley dropped us off and said he was going to be right back. Man, this nigga did not even come back until an hour after the party. Calvin and I were ready to whup yo ass, Mo!"

Moseley just grinned as he drove down Overhill and turned right on Slauson. He looked at the clock. It was 9:48. "By ten-thirty, I'm going to be at the party with Natasha," he said.

I knew that was not true because we got to the party at 10:15. It would not take Moseley fifteen minutes to get from Inglewood to Watts and back to Inglewood again. He wasn't the fastest driver in LA. Moseley let us out of the car in front of the building.

"I'll be back," he promised.

"Yeah, yeah whatever," Anthony said, slamming the car door shut.

Anthony and I walked into the party dressed for the occasion, stunning females left and right. Anthony looked like a celebrity, dressed in a Paul Smith hoodie with Rock & Republic jeans. He completed the ensemble with some fresh Creative Recreation sneakers, clean and color-coordinated.

"Damn, I see some material up in here," he said, referring to the fly girls in the party that were dancing and socializing.

I could do nothing but agree as I saw absolutely gorgeous girls that caught my eye. I know there was one or more females that I wanted to take down by the end of the night. I posted up on the wall, feeling clean and looking fresh. Anthony looked at me like I was crazy.

"What, Ant?" I asked him, giving him the same crazy look he was giving me.

"What are you doing?" Anthony asked.

"Nigga . . . I'm posted up checkin' out these females," I answered.

Anthony shook his head. "Khalid, you been in jail too damn long. We don't post up waiting for a female to come by so we can pull her arm. We're ladies' men! We get active with these ladies up close and personal. C'mon nigga, we're goin' to dance," Anthony informed.

Anthony and I went into the crowd, snagging two females as we went in. We were across from each other, each with a girl in front of us dancing her ass off. Anthony had this dark-skinned model-looking chick who must have had some Jamaican in her the way she winded her hips. I had a pretty light-skinned girl performing the classic pretty-girl dance—"too fly to work it out but not too pretty to not dance." She wasn't dancing too hard for me. She probably didn't want to sweat out the tight curls in her hair. I grabbed her hand, pulled her into me, and wrapped my arm tighter around her waist. She eventually loosened up and arched her back as she rotated her waist and ass in a circular motion. She shook her hips from left to right and soon I had a hard-on.

As if he was sparing me, the DJ put on Ginuwine's "Pony," our oldie but goodie. My dancer opened up her legs and put her hands on her knees. She rolled her waist and put that ass on me in a way so crucial that I had to have her by the end of the night.

"I see you, Khalid," Anthony cheered me on as his wind-

ing cutie continued to drop it on him. We shook hands
above their heads. The song faded out and Anthony stepped
back from the girl.

Expecting me to do the same, Anthony beckoned me to
him. I told him to hold on while I got another dance. Anthony excused me from the girl and dragged me away.

"Damn, Anthony," I groaned. "That girl is fine!"

"Peep the game, my nigga," Anthony began. "Don't
cling to them. If opportunity comes again, we will get their
number. Don't dance with the same girl."

"Damn, I been locked up for a minute and I come back
to hear 'How To Run Game 101' from you," I laughed.
"Anthony, let me do this my way."

Anthony shrugged his shoulders. "If you insist," he said.
"But you'll be better off with my plan."

I walked back over to my light-skinned desire. She was
talking with her friend when another guy came up from behind and grabbed her. She gave her friend a wild, confused
look. Her friend shrugged her shoulders. To save her from
an unwanted dance, I approached them and took her away
from her.

"Ay, I got this," I said to him. He nodded and walked
away. "You know him?"

She shook her head. "Hell, nah I don't know him. That
fool is probably drunk or high!" she whined. "Grabbing
me like that? He's on something for sure!"

I wrapped her arms around my neck and put mine
around her waist. "Damn, you are beautiful." Even though
I was spitting game, I was being dead honest.

She smiled bashfully, holding her head down. "Thank
you," she responded. "You got a name?"

"Khalid," I answered.

"Khalid," she repeated. "What does that mean, my
brother?"

"It's Arabic and it means *immortal*," I answered. "And no, I am not Muslim."

"Immortal, I like that. Do you consider yourself immortal?"

"By all means, no. Though it does seem like I've lived nine lives," I replied. "What's your name?"

"Kiani," she said. "Straight outta Baldwin Hills." She giggled.

"Really, now?" I said, assuming she was privileged with two working parents in the home, definitely educated but probably knew nothing of the hood. She was already special in my book.

"So where do you go to school?" Kiani asked. "Oh immortal one?"

"I'm not in school," I answered. "But where do you go to school?"

"I go to Loyola Marymount University."

"LMU girl. You must be smart."

"Yeah, something like that," Kiani laughed. "No college for you?"

"Does that bother you?"

Kiani laughed. "Well, you're cute so I can't say that it does."

"So when are you going to let me get your number or should I give you mine and you call me whenever?"

Kiani blushed, making me view her as a shy but sexy girl. "Take your pick," she quietly whispered.

My mind set went straight to the gutter and I began thinking suggestive thoughts. "Take my pick?" I repeated. She nodded. "I'm going to give you my number and I can only hope that you call me whenever." She took out her cell phone and I put the house number under "Immortal." Hopefully when she called she would remember my real name.

I looked back at Anthony who was at this point laughing at me. I told Kiani I would be back later. Hesitantly, she said okay and turned me loose. *Who's clinging now?* I thought. I walked over to Anthony who was conversing with another homeboy about me. Anthony stuck out his hand for me to shake.

"I must give it to you. That one was in the bag," he said.

"And I was able to do it playing my game. I didn't need your advice," I bragged.

Anthony chuckled. "Well, you sure needed it when it came to clothes."

Anthony was the softer one of the group, but still had our respect because of his upbeat personality. He was an ideal ladies' man thanks to his ability to sing, love for R&B, and his charm. We often used some of his lines because they really worked. We encouraged him to write a book with Dior! *Men Versus Women: Who Plays The Game Better?* It's still in the works. Anthony could screw a girl over, and sing his way back into forgiveness. What young man wouldn't envy that? Anthony, overall, was one hell of a friend who I had to keep around.

Our conversation came to a halt when three people I never planned on running into tonight came through the door: Rock, Pablo, and Aaron.

"You got to be kidding me," I said thinking out loud.

"What? I did help you with your outfit!" Anthony said, on the wrong page.

"I'm not talking about that," I answered. "Three mark-ass niggas just came into the party." An exhausting sigh escaped from my mouth from just thinking about the possibilities that could occur now that these boys were here.

"Who are you talking about?" Anthony asked.

"Pablo, Rock, and Aaron," I answered.

Anthony swallowed the lump in his throat. If I happened to get into a confrontation with my ex-homeboys, Anthony was the wrong one to be with. Here was a time where I needed Calvin and Moseley.

"I sure hope they don't start no shit," Anthony said, wiping beads of sweat from his forehead.

"Yeah, but in case they do," I began, "you gon' be ready?"

"I guess so," Anthony replied.

Not quite the answer I was looking for, but it would do.

Even though the three people I despised the most were in the same facility as me, I refused to let it ruin my good time. After all, this was the first party I had been to in three years. I had missed out on so much being locked up, and partying was one of the things I missed out on. I'm not one to let a good moment slip away, and I remembered I had some unfinished business with Kiani.

I made my way over to her, standing in the same spot I left her.

"So you came back?" she asked, somewhat surprised.

"Yeah," I answered, grabbing her hands. We began to sway to the music, holding hands and looking into each other's eyes. "I'm a man of my word."

"That's good to know," Kiani said. "What are you doing later?"

"He's gon'na be with his boys," answered the voice, not mine.

I looked to my left and saw Rock, Pablo, and Aaron, each giving me cold stares as if they were trying to ruin my good time.

"Well, Hide, it's a coincidence I ran into you," Rock began. "The big homies was just asking about you the other day."

"Yeah, like where you been hiding and why you haven't shown your face around the hood," Pablo continued.

Aaron butted in and said, "Niggas starting to think you turned your back or some shit."

My eyes met Kiani's. She was clueless as to what was going on and wanted to stay that way. She told me she would call me soon and dismissed herself quietly. I watched her walk over to a friend and turned my attention back to the Van Ness Gangsters.

"Look muthafuckas," I said angrily, my fist balled up so tight that my nails dug into my skin. "The hood turned they back on me, so I have every right to say the hell with you niggas. I'm doing me . . . and that don't include running back to Van Ness Gangsters tryna put in work. The only work I'm putting in is for me. Tell the big homies I said that."

"Oh, you think it's that easy?" Pablo asked.

"I know I can't just walk away from the hood without some drama along the way, but watch me," I said looking them up and down, returning that same cold stare they were giving me.

"You shoulda thought about that before you got put on blood," Aaron said.

I shrugged my shoulders and replied, "Yeah, but I didn't, so now what?"

"Nigga, whatchu wanna do?" Pablo asked. "Those sound like fighting words to me."

"It's whatever," I said. I knew the deal and knew the drill, and expected Pablo to be the one to start a fight. I was ready. There was no backing down. I was my own hood . . . and I had to defend it if I wanted my respect. The one thing Van Ness Gangsters would have to do is respect me and my decision to quit gangbanging, and I'd fight for that right.

Rock cooled his boy down by saying, "Chill, Pablo. He'll have to deal with us one way or the other. Now ain't the time."

"You damn right. Y'all gon' have to deal with me," I added.

Our conversation ended there. Rock, Pablo, and Aaron walked off into the crowd. Moseley ran up behind me.

"Ay, them niggas tryna get out there?" he said, ready to fight.

"Nah," I answered. "But I'm ready in case they were. You jus got here?"

"Yeah, Natasha got a lil' attitude so I'm pissed I brought her here and it's all these bad-ass females in here," Moseley said, scoping out the ladies in the room. "Definitely shoulda left her ass in Watts."

Natasha emerged from the crowd to find Moseley standing next to me. "There you are. Mo, I'm starting to think you don't want me here. Why you keep running off?"

"Didn't I tell you I had to see what was up with the homie? Khalid, Natasha. Natasha, this is Khalid," Moseley introduced.

"Hi, Khalil'," was the swift reply.

"It's Khalid, babe," Moseley corrected.

"My bad."

"Don't trip," I told her.

"I'll catch you after the party," Moseley said, following Natasha onto the dance floor.

I nodded and made my way over to Anthony, who had become the life of the party.

"You enjoying yourself, man?" he asked me, isolating himself from the crowd.

"I am," I said, meaning each word.

Just having the freedom to be out was enjoyable. There was no "in bed by eight," no "three simple meals a day," and there was no sound of the jail gates slamming shut. This same freedom that others took for granted, was the same freedom I appreciated—and wouldn't let anyone or anything take away from me again.

Chapter Five

Shay

"Hello?" Her raspy morning voice brought back old memories of me calling her in the early morning three years ago.

"Good morning beautiful," I greeted her. "You up yet?"

"Does it sound like it?" was Shay's rude reply. "Who is this?"

Her unawareness shattered me. She should've recognized my voice like how she used to way back. "Khalid," I answered.

"Oh, nah, I wasn't up yet," she told me.

"You want me to call you later then?" I asked.

"No, there's no point now. I'm up now, thanks to you," She answered. "What are you doing up so early?"

"Early? It's only seven in the morning," I said sarcastically.

"On a Sunday?" Shay asked. "Please! God don't even get up this early on a Sunday. I hope you're getting up early to go to church."

"Nah, I'm not," I said. "But I do want to take you to breakfast."

"Aw, if you're paying?"

"C'mon now, you know I ain't got no money. How am I supposed to pay?" I asked.

"Don't be a cheap ass," Shay said.

"All right, I'll be over there around ten. So you got three hours," I said. We got off the phone. I walked out the living room and knocked on Calvin's bedroom door. I heard him get out of bed and walk over to the door, opening it slowly.

"Yeah, man?" he said groggily.

"Damn, what's up with y'all? Y'all ain't morning people? It's seven o'clock," I said. I was used to waking up early from the prison guard's yells and baton banging on the jail bars at six-thirty in the morning. My body alarm clock had adjusted to the routine and I've been a morning person ever since.

"It's too damn early in the morning. What do you want?" asked an irritated Calvin.

"Let me hold a dub," I said. "I'll get you back as soon as I can."

"Why?" Calvin asked, opening his door wider. He returned back to the bed, falling flat on his stomach.

I stood in the doorway. "I'm taking Shay out to eat for breakfast. You know I don't have a job yet, so I'm a little broke."

"Well, take her out when you got a job," Calvin said.

"C'mon, man. Let me get a twenty," I asked Calvin once more.

"Real shit, though. I don't have twenty. So ask Mo," he said. "And close my door on the way out!"

I slammed his door shut purposely. I went across the hall to Moseley's room. I walked right in and wished I hadn't. Moseley was lying on his bed butt naked with no covers. I quickly shielded my eyes.

"Damn, Moseley! Put on some clothes," I said, rushing back out of the room.

"That's what you get for running up in here like that," Moseley laughed. "Next time knock."

"Just let me hold a twenty," I stated.

"I can't," Moseley said.

"Why the hell not?"

" 'cuz I gotta use it on gas and gas ain't cheap," he answered. "A lot of things changed while you were locked up . . . including the price of gas, god damn it!"

"Damn, Mo! I'm trying to take Shay out for breakfast," I said, pleading my case. "You don't have nothing?"

"Well, you shouldn't offer to take a girl out if you ain't got no money to spend her, rule number twenty-nine," said a sarcastic Moseley.

I rolled my eyes and went into the living room to see Anthony snoring loudly on the couch opposite the one I slept on. I didn't even feel like bothering him. I went into the bathroom to get washed up and ready for the day.

I put some Neutrogena soap on my face—and believe it or not, it works for men. For the longest I believed it was strictly a women's product due to commercials and advertisements. It wasn't until Anthony convinced me that bath products shouldn't be specifically for men or women that I agreed and used the product that kept pimples off my face and exfoliated my skin. Once again, I had learned something from the man who showered with Victoria Secret's amber romance shower gel. Anthony was all about breaking the rules, in more ways than one.

I took a long, hot shower, anticipating my morning with Shay. After ten minutes, I wrapped a towel around my lower half and stepped out of the shower. I brushed my teeth making sure each was sparkling and my breath was minty fresh.

By time I had got dressed and stepped out of the bathroom, the house had picked up quite a lot. Calvin was up watching ESPN. Anthony was sorting through his clothes in the hallway closet. Moseley, dressed in Hush Puppie slippers and a robe, was cleaning his room with the door wide open. Dior was in the kitchen cooking breakfast dressed in Sunday's best. She looked like a black conservative housewife and I had to laugh.

"What's so funny?" Dior asked.

"You!" I replied as if the answer was obvious. "You a housewife now?"

Dior shook her head. "Whatever, Khalid. You hungry?"

"Yeah, let me get a pancake and two slices of bacon," I answered.

"You call that hungry?" she asked in response. "You just ordered a kid's meal."

I chuckled and asked, "Oh yeah, do you think I can hold a twenty?"

"What do you need a twenty for?" Dior asked, ceasing her cooking.

"I'm taking ya girl Shay out for breakfast."

"With no money?" Dior asked, confused with my decision to take Shay out with no money to pay for the meal. She went into her purse and took out her wallet. "How soon can you pay me back?"

"As soon as I get a job," I answered.

Dior replied drily, "And when will that be?"

"Soon," I said, smirking.

Dior laughed and handed me twenty-five dollars. "I only need twenty," I said, refusing the extra five dollars.

"Tax," she informed me. "Take it."

"Thanks, Dior. Sorry I have to borrow money from you, but you know I really like Shay. I want us to get back on track. Calvin, Mo, and Ant couldn't help a brotha out. But thanks again," I said, humbled by the loan.

"No problem," Dior kindly replied. "I know you and

Shay are good friends. I'm sure she'll enjoy the breakfast 'cuz that girl can eat! Y'all have a good time!"

With that being said, I took the money and put it in my pocket as Dior put her wallet back in her purse. Calvin walked in the kitchen, just in time to her putting away the wallet. He slapped his hand on my shoulder, a friendly but rough gesture.

"I see you got ya money," he said. "I wonder how." He gave Dior a disapproving look.

She put her head down as if she knew she was in trouble. She frowned and almost jumped when he tapped her on the arm. He told her to follow him into the room—he had something to show her.

Dior and Calvin went into the room and he turned around to face her. He put his hands on his hips and shook his head. "Did you ask if you could loan Khalid some money?"

She shook her head and replied, "Sorry, but I didn't know I had to ask you what to do with my money."

"What the hell you mean you didn't know? You should already know you suppose to ask me about stuff like that. How can you loan money to my boy but not to me? You get mad when I ask!" Calvin said. "Asking me stupid questions like 'don't you got a job' and shit!"

"Khalid is my friend too! And he doesn't have a job—"

"So how is he supposed to pay you back?"

"Watch who you're yelling at!"

"I yell at you all the time! Why you tripping now?"

"Calvin, don't start with me this morning!" Dior hollered.

They argued with such emotion I thought they were going to emerge into the hallway in a fight. I got out of my seat after hearing the conversation that was supposed to be between the couple and went into the room. I handed Dior the money back.

"What are you doing, Khalid? You can keep it," she said, confused by the return.

"Nah, I'm good," I answered. "Your man probably needs it more than I do." I made sure to make eye contact with Calvin when saying *your man*.

Calvin gave me a cold, hard stare that would've been taken as a challenge any other day. I didn't have the time to address it. Calvin was on some stupid shit anyway. I'd let that be Dior's problem. I turned my back on him and walked away.

I didn't want to be in the house any longer after that. I scooped up Anthony's weekly bus pass and headed out of the door. I caught the bus to Shay's house, which took about fifteen minutes of my time.

I walked about two blocks down from the bus stop until I got to her house. I saw her outside watering her mother's city garden, which consisted of sun-dried flowers, weeds, and short grass. She wore denim shorts, a shirt that said *I'm Way Cuter Than Your Girlfriend* and some Vans tennis shos. She turned around and looked at me.

"Hey, Khalid," Shay said, tossing the water pot aside. She gave me a hug and continued, "And how are you doing?"

"Good," I said, surprised at how nice she was acting toward me. This was the complete opposite of her morning crankiness.

"Come on, let's get inside," she said hurriedly. "Where are we going to eat?" She opened the front door and proceeded into the living room.

I followed her inside and answered, "I would like to go to Roscoe's, but I wasn't able to get any money. We could just go and leave without paying." I tried not to let my embarrassment show on my face. This feeling of being broke was just a confirmation that I needed to get a job and soon.

It would take some time, especially with a record like mine, but I was determined to get one.

"You're kidding," she said with a dry look. I shook my head. "How about this, Khalid. Why don't I just cook some breakfast for us? That way we save my money and my time."

"That's cool, as long as you don't kill me," I said humorously.

"Ah, you got jokes!" She laughed and went into the kitchen. She talked loud enough for me to still hear her in another room. "So how are things now that you're back?"

"Crazy as ever," I said. "Do you know they can't even get up in the morning?"

Shay giggled and replied, "Khalid, this isn't jail. We don't get up at six in the morning."

"Oh, so *you* got jokes now? That's all right, Shay. Don't cook me too much food. You might hurt yourself."

"Um, was that a joke? Good one," Shay said, making the sarcasm in her tone very apparent.

I would have hit her with another joke, but I couldn't. I stared at a glamorous picture of her hanging on the wall in the living room. I was taken aback by her beauty. She made me forget what it was I was about to say next—she was so gorgeous. Aging three years had done her good. She was fuller, more radiant—she was a woman. It was her physical beauty alone that made my barriers crumble when I was around her. I knew I still had feelings for her and wouldn't try to hide them. "Hey Shay," I said, changing the subject. "You ever get those two letters I wrote you from jail?"

"Yes, I did."

"Why didn't you write back then?" I asked as I got up and walked into the kitchen to see her. She was so beautiful and her beauty was something I had to see. I felt like a young boy in love with the girl next door because I was becoming infatuated with her . . . all over again.

"I did write back," Shay said as she cracked an egg into the glass bowl.

"Well, I didn't get the letter."

"That's because I never sent it," Shay replied. "Look in my room, in the top drawer of my dresser . . . toward the right-hand side in the back."

I went into her bedroom and followed her exact directions to finding the letter that was never sent to me. Her lacy underwear was stacked neatly on the left side, and on the right side were different shades of 36 C bras. I gently lifted the bras and saw a letter addressed to LA county jail. My name was above the address. I took the letter, replaced the bras, and closed the drawer. I returned to the kitchen where Shay was now cutting open a roll of Jimmy Dean sausage.

"So why didn't you send me the letter, Shay?" I inquired.

She was quiet for a couple of seconds, concentrating on her meal. She shrugged her shoulders and said, "I had forgotten all about it."

"That's bullshit," I said. "So how the hell did it end up in your drawer? And where are the letters I gave you?"

Shay said, "I put them there." Something about the way she said it indicated there was another story behind it.

"They are in my drawer on the left side," she answered slowly. "I read them."

"Well, it's too bad I couldn't read yours. I really could have used that behind bars, Shay," I told her, truthfully. "For a minute I really thought you lost contact with a nigga. I was just asking myself what I did wrong and how I hurt you. I didn't know what to think."

Shay took a deep breath before speaking again, searching for the right words to say. "I wanted to send them, I really did," she answered in a low voice.

"Why didn't you?" I asked her as I fanned the letter into my open hand.

Shay grabbed a spatula and flipped the pink and brown sausage over. She never made eye contact with me once she began to speak. "It was just one of those things where I backed out. Wrote the letter, sealed it and put a stamp on it. I never found the courage to place it in the mailbox."

"Never found the courage?" I repeated. Lord knows I was scared about a lot of things, but one of them was never writing Shay a letter.

"It took a lot for me to write that letter, Khalid. You know I don't just put my emotions out there. I was angry with you for going back to jail. I know we weren't . . . together as a couple, but I did care a lot about you. And when you got locked up, it hit me hard. These past three years I've did a lot of growing up."

I had noticed. Shay wasn't that teenage girl I couldn't let go of anymore. She was a woman. I would get a better understanding of her and who she had become over the past three years after reading her letter, which I couldn't wait to do.

Shay finished cooking our breakfast, and sat a plate of sausage, eggs, grits, and two thick pancakes with butter melting over it on the table before me. She poured me a glass of orange juice and made herself a plate. We spent the conversation catching up on the past three years.

"So where's your family at?" I asked her while cutting into my hot pancakes.

"They spent the weekend at Disneyland and the hotel. They'll be home later on tonight," Shay answered.

"Why didn't you go?" I asked.

" 'cuz I had to pack up. I go back to school tomorrow. Dior and I leave out tomorrow morning. Vacation is over now," Shay said.

"Where y'all go to school again?"

"Cal State University San Bernadino!" she screeched, proud of her school.

"You like it?"

"Yeah, it's cool," Shay answered. "So what do you plan to do now that you're back?"

"Definitely find a job. I'll probably enroll at West LA College," I said. "Get an AA degree in something."

"Good plan. You know you gotta put all that gangbanging shit to the side though," Shay said in a caring tone.

"Yeah, I know. It doesn't matter. I don't fuck with my old niggas any more. Those niggas did me dirty. I'm over that shit, though," I responded.

"Well, don't get put on another hood either. I know you hang with a lot of dem boys from 20's. Running with the crippled will make you limp," Shay said, almost sounding like a mother.

"I believe it," I said. "So how has love been for you?"

Shay frowned as if the topic was touchy. I asked her again as if she didn't hear me, though I knew she did. "It's been all right. I ain't in it or nothing."

"So do you have a boyfriend?" I asked.

"Khalid, I told you I wasn't in love!"

"But you didn't tell me if you had a boyfriend or not. Just 'cuz you ain't in love don't mean you don't have a boyfriend," I stated. "So now, do you have a boyfriend?"

"Something like that," she answered hesitantly.

"Something like that?" I repeated. "Shay, you and I both know that doesn't make any type of sense."

"Yes, Khalid. I have a boyfriend," she answered. "Nyrique."

Nyrique? I repeated the name in my head over and over again. I only knew of one Nyrique—and he and I, let's just say, weren't the best of friends. Hell, we weren't the least of friends. "Nyrique King? Is he from 30s?"

Shay's eyes lit up with surprise and shock. "You know Nyrique? How?"

"We had a run-in way back in the day," I said remembering the time he boldly came up to Fairfax High School to pick up his friend Tito.

A couple of mean mugs were exchanged, followed by some gang signs. Nyrique stepped out of the car with his two homeboys. Out the corner of my eye I saw Tito coming from behind me. Tito passed me by and got into the car. They drove off and managed to throw up some gang signs and the middle finger up as they did.

When the Black Expo came around at the Los Angeles Convention Center, my hood and Nyrique's hood got into a huge fight. Guns popped off and it resulted in a loss of one of their people. That was the last I saw of Nyrique because I ended up going back to jail.

"So you're dating a crip?" I asked.

"Why does it matter? I'm not with you," Shay replied. She put a hot spoon of grits in her mouth and washed it down with some pulp-free orange juice.

"I suppose that was meant to hurt me," I said. "But it didn't."

"I don't know what does."

"You tryna say I don't have any feelings?"

Shay raised her eyebrows, slowly rolled her eyes, and said, "Well—"

"I got feelings, Shay. Hell, I had feelings for you. Why people think a black man don't care about shit? I care about a lot of things."

"Khalid, don't sit up here and give me your version of *Men Cry In The Dark*. You want to prove something to me and the world? Prove that you can stay out of jail," Shay spat coldly.

"Damn, I go to jail with you as a friend and get out with

you as my mama? One minute everything is good and the next you on your period!" I yelled back at her.

"How did we even get on this topic?" Shay mumbled.

"Yeah, I thought we were talking about Nyrique. How is that going?" I asked.

Shay asked, "Why do you care?"

I shrugged my shoulders and said, "I think the question is why *should* I care?"

Without saying another word, I finished off every breakfast item on my plate and drank the glass of orange juice that came with it. I used the napkin to wipe my mouth.

"Thanks for the breakfast, Shay." Even though the conversation went cold after the Nyrique subject, I was going to end the morning peacefully. "It feels good to have a home-cooked breakfast."

"You're welcome," Shay replied. "So . . . are you going to read that letter I wrote?"

"Should I read it?" I wanted to hear her reply.

Shay shook her head, and I wasn't surprised. "No, I don't think I'm ready to let you see it . . . yet," she answered.

"All right, I'll just put it back in your drawer," I told her.

I went into her room, opened the drawer, and looked on the left side under the panties. I saw my letters. I took them out. They had been opened. I placed them back in the drawer, along with her letter to me. At this point, I had to follow the rule that "some things are better left unsaid." Whatever Shay had written in the letter to me just wasn't meant for me to read. I wouldn't let her know that I wanted to read it, felt I needed to read it, and was upset with her for not letting me do so. On top of all that, Shay had a boyfriend. Nyrique King. Someone from my past who I didn't get along with, not for any personal reason but because of the laws of the street. He's a crip, I used to be a blood. And even if I did see him again, we wouldn't be friends only because of Shay. Another man had who I wanted to be my girl. Wanted to be . . .

But after this breakfast with Shay, I knew where I stood with her. We'd never be together. I hugged Shay good-bye and left her house for the bus stop, feeling it was evident what Shay had done to our relationship. She took it and put it away, buried underneath something else, planning to never return to it again.

Chapter Six

Dior

I almost didn't want to pick up the house phone seeing that is was Dior . . . once again calling for Calvin. It was only twenty minute ago that she had called looking for him. I picked up again to tell her Calvin still had not made it home.

"Sorry to call again, Khalid. Calvin still not in?" Dior asked with hope in her voice that her man had arrived home.

"Nope, not yet. Have you tried his cell phone? He might answer the cell," I suggested to her.

"His cell phone is off," Dior answered. "I'm just worried."

"What happened?" I asked, assuming the couple was going through the monthly turmoil.

"Nothing, really. He just hasn't called me yet. And it feels weird," Dior answered.

"You got an intuition or something?" I asked.

"I don't know. Can an intuition be wrong?"

"That intuition is a dangerous thing," I answered. "Sometimes you women get so caught up in thoughts of your man cheating that you actually start to believe them."

Dior hissed, "Shit, what am I asking you for? You're a guy. Only women have that intuition."

"It may not be intuition. It's probably insecurity. You tend to do that often, Dior."

"Well, Calvin made me this way. I don't think he knows I know. But he has cheated on me before. How do I know he's not going to do it again?" Dior asked.

"You don't," I replied.

"So what am I supposed to do?"

"Take it easy and trust him in the meantime."

Dior agreed and said, "Yes, I suppose you are right. Well, if he comes in, tell him I'm at the dorms and to give me a call."

Twenty minutes there was still no Calvin and another call from Dior coming in.

"Hello? Calvin?" she said when I answered the phone.

"No, Dior. It's Khalid," I replied. "You're looking for your man?"

"Yes, I am," she said forwardly.

I also heard worry in her voice. From that, I knew she was coming out with a series of questions after I told her he wasn't at the house.

"He's not here yet," I answered, preparing myself for the reasonable-doubt questions that were boarding her brain.

"Khalid, can I ask you a few questions?"

"Shoot," I allowed her. I pretended that this "questionnaire" was sudden, but I'd studied Dior and her position in the relationship so her moves were predictable.

"Does Calvin have females calling the house?"

"No," I lied. "At least not when I pick up the phone," when in actuality, three other females called for Calvin, but they were friends. I knew that for sure.

"Hmm," Dior moaned as if she knew I was lying. "I find that hard to believe. Has he told you about any experiences with other women?"

C'mon Dior, if it was him asking the questions I wouldn't rat you out, I thought to myself. I fibbed, "No, he didn't, Dior."

She sucked her teeth out of anger from not finding out any information. "Well, do you think Calvin is cheating?"

Not anymore, I wanted to say. But I couldn't! If Dior found out Calvin used to cheat—not that her common sense hadn't already told her—it wasn't going to be from my mouth. "Nah, I think he's crazy about you. If he ain't at work or with you, then he's at Evan's house. What could he and Evan possibly do? All they do is smoke and play video games." I stated what I knew . . . or at least what I hoped was true.

"You can't be too sure."

"Obviously, neither can you."

Dior, if I'm not mistaken, sobbed and blew her nose.

"What's that supposed to mean?"

"Why are you so insecure?" I asked.

"How many times have I heard that before?" she asked herself out loud.

"And how many times have you been honest?" I decided to throw in for more realization.

She answered apologetically, "I know, and I'm sorry about it. I don't mean to be insecure. I really don't! But I can't afford to have him cheat on me again."

"Again?" I asked.

"Yes, again. I know he's cheated on me before."

"How did you find out?"

"It was when I was doing my senior year up north in the Bay area. High school years," Dior responded. "I don't want to go through that again. I really don't want to."

I felt sorry for her. I knew this was why she allowed herself to become Calvin's every necessity. By stepping down from her given authority, she hoped to keep Calvin from running around. Many guys would love to have a young woman like Dior who abided by their rules. But at what cost? And why must the woman pay?

"Khalid? You there?" she asked me.

I had spaced out for about a couple of seconds and she had gotten lonely. "Yes, I am. Look, Dior. I know for a fact Calvin loves you. He ain't cheating. Is he showing any signs?"

"I can't really say. It's the little stuff like not calling me back when he says or when he's supposed to," Dior answered.

"Okay, well, people get sidetracked. You know that. Use common sense over insecurity. It's bad if people notice it from the outside."

"All right."

"And another thing, don't let Calvin talk to you like you're a little kid. It's not cool the way he comes at you," I said, feeling it was necessary to inform her about the way Calvin talked to her. It bothered me to see another young man, especially my friend, talk down to their woman.

"I don't think he means to talk to me like that. He just gets angry, you know?"

"No, I don't know, because I don't talk down to a woman no matter how mad I am. And don't tell me what you think. You're blind to it because you're in love with Calvin. You're so in love that you'd do anything for him," I said, showing her nothing shy of tough love.

She snickered. "We'll, excuse me. Somebody should receive the 'Tupac of the Year' award!"

"I can't help the fact that I respect all females no matter where they come from or where they're going. And some of them don't deserve to be respected at all, now do they?"

I replied. "Now promise me that you will stand up for yourself and find a backbone!"

Dior laughed and it warmed me to know I made her smile at a time it was needed. "You got my word!" she said.

Timing is everything. Right when I was going to end the conversation, Calvin walked in the door. "What a coincidence! Here's Calvin." I tossed him the phone.

He caught it and put the phone on speaker as he went into the room. "Hello?"

"Hey boo!" Dior chimed. "Where ya been?"

I could still hear every word of the conversation.

"Evan's," Calvin answered.

"Shoulda known. You didn't pick up your cell when I called. Why?" Dior asked.

"I was playing Madden," Calvin said.

"Why didn't you call after you lost?" she asked, trying to add humor to the situation, only she felt serious. "And then the phone went straight to voice mail when I tried to call again."

"We went to smoke, and my phone battery went dead. I'm putting it on the charger right now. What were you and Khalid talking about?" Calvin asked, changing the subject. He trailed into the bathroom.

"Nothing. I just called," Dior lied.

"You sure?"

"Um . . . yeah."

"Why does the phone indicate that y'all been talking for seven minutes?"

"Calvin?"

"What were y'all talking about?"

"Nothing, really. Just college."

"College? For Khalid?"

"No, he was asking me how things were going at San Bernadino."

Calvin was skeptical, but didn't let it faze him. "Right,

Dior. If I'm not here when you call, just hang up. You understand me?"

"I understand," Dior responded.

I figured some shit just has to slide to keep the one you
love.

Chapter Seven

Kiani

Kiani dug her nails into my back as my manhood crept inside her. She moaned and the warmth of her breath against my ear resulted in goose bumps. It was surreal to me because I hadn't had some good pussy in years and I'm not one to beat my meat from photographed arousal. My hand ran through her hair and I noticed it was not a weave. Her legs wrapped around my torso as I inched deeper into her with every grunt.

She began panting and I hadn't even pulled out. I felt like cumming because after thirty minutes or so of good sex, I could no longer hold out. I lifted her up off of my dick and released. She licked my neck like an overjoyed puppy lapping at its newfound owner.

"Damn, boy," she breathed heavily. "I'm not going to lie. That was the best dick I've had in a long time. Shit, that's the only dick I had in a long time."

I found the strength to smile though I wanted to pass out, but I didn't. I held my composure and acted cool. "What can I say? You got some good stuff too, Kiani."

She laughed and asked me, "What are your plans for later on today?"

I shrugged and said, "I don't know. Why? You want to hang out?"

"Well, I have my Saturday class at ten today. If you wanna come back to my crib for round two then you can."

I thought before answering. I didn't want to sneak in through her window like I did at six o'clock this morning. The things I do for a little hit. Kiani suggested I come in the morning because her mom and dad were dead asleep. So I woke up around six, caught the bus to Baldwin Hills, and walked to her upper-class home in the Black Beverly Hills. If this kept up, I'd eventually drop her because I shouldn't have to schedule pussy.

"I might be able to," I answered. "But I'm going to the mall to look for a job so I'll call you later if I'm not going to make it."

"What mall are you going to?"

"The Fox Hills Mall."

"Well, that's on the way to my class at West LA. Let's get round two in and you can come with me. You'll just sneak out the window, go down the street, and I'll be right behind in the car."

"Nice plan," I said, referring to her round two rather than me catching a ride with her.

Kiani and I went at it one more time. After the second release, Kiani allowed me to shower with her in her bathroom, linked into her bedroom. I left the bathroom with a towel covering around my lower half. I had a moment to think.

First off, though Kiani was well worth me creeping through a window, I didn't want to do this for the remainder of our relationship. If she was going to have me over, she would need to introduce me to her parents so I could use the proper entrance, the front door. Secondly, I had to find a job and with the record of being in jail three times, my chances were slim. But I could only blame myself for the setback because I was the idiot who did the stupid actions that got me in the situation I was in. I could admit it, and that was the problem with some of these brothers out of jail. They could not admit their mistakes.

Kiani was dressed in a tight-hugging white tee and some form-fitting jeans with sandals. "Are you ready?" she asked, grabbing her designer handbag.

"Yeah," I said and followed her out the door.

"No, Khalid. You have to sneak out the window and I'll get you at the corner," she said, stopping me dead in my tracks.

"Kiani, your parents are still asleep. And your house is huge, girl! Let me walk out with you," I said. "I'm not a criminal anymore. I don't sneak in and out of people's homes anymore."

"What?" Kiani asked, thrown off by my last remark.

"Why can't I walk out the front door? If your folks are still asleep they won't even know I'm here," I said, trying my hardest to get her to change her mind about having me hop through the window.

"I don't want to take the risk." Kiani wouldn't budge.

I rolled my eyes and turned around, heading back toward the room. I hopped out the window landing on the outside of her house in the driveway. I dodged down the avenue and waited for Kiani to drive up behind me. She pulled up next to the curb and I hopped in the passenger side of the car.

We drove to the Fox Hills Mall where Kiani dropped me off. Before I could get out the car, she flung her arms around my neck. "So I'll see you later?" she asked, close to my ear.

"Hopefully," I said with uncertainty.

"Mmm, okay," she said.

One more kiss was given before I got out of the car. "Happy job hunting!" she said.

I shook my head and closed the car door. She drove off and I realized that Kiani just may be too sweet to let go so soon.

Chapter Eight

Moseley

Moseley set the football down on the grass of King Park while staring down some crips from Harlem. Evil glances made their way across the field of grass. Moseley and Jordan noticed each one.

Moseley got most of his newfound attitude and gangsta ego from Jordan, who had been gangbanging since the age of eleven and claimed it was hereditary. His father was a thug and his grandfather was a Black Panther. The rebellious attitude was hereditary, but somehow the cause shifted gears over the decades. Jordan was a slang-talking, gangbanging, money-hungry, trigger-happy, respect-needing, power-driven thug who abided by the rules of the street.

The people around him felt he had gotten so far into his deadly lifestyle that there was no changing him. The miracle would have to be performed by God; therefore his family had depended solely on prayer for his coming out. But faith without works is dead and Jordan had no desire to change.

Jordan did not listen and instead went with his street demand to prove his manliness or his gangsta. Jordan walked toward the seven crips. He didn't recognize all the eternal damage that was bound to come with this confrontation. Moseley saw this taking a deadly turn. He didn't want to leave Jordan hanging, and instead of going toward his car he took slow steps toward Jordan and the crips.

Three (or more) words sealed Jordan's fate. Moseley watched in horror as one of the crips took out a .44-caliber and pierced Jordan's chest with the bullets. Moseley ran toward the confrontation with his own handgun drawn out. He fired at the crips; one fired back at Moseley still charging toward them. A bullet grazed him in his arm and he fell to the ground. He bled slowly and held onto his wound, looking up at the light blue sky and cotton ball resembling clouds.

The crips fled from the scene of the murder to safety. It was over as soon as it started. Moseley felt as if the scattering of their feet rumbled the earth's floor. It was like a mini earthquake was happening as he closed his eyes, and wished that when he opened them he'd be a home and Jordan would still be alive.

A few moments later, when the coast was clear and he was able to move freely without the worry of the crips returning to finish him off, Moseley took out his cell phone. He wanted to cry from the pain of the bullet wound in his stomach. He was bleeding a lot. He managed to call 911, and then home.

"Hello?"

"Who is this?"

"Khalid. Who is this?"

"Mo nigga, I got shot."

"You got hit bad?"

"The bullet hit my stomach, but I'm gon" be okay. This shit does sting, though!"

"Who was with you?"

"Jordan."

"He okay?"

"Nope, he got shot in the chest. I think he's dead. Damn, man."

"Fuck!" Khalid exclaimed. "Okay, where you at?"

"I'm at King Park."

"I'm on the way."

"I called the police and they're sending an ambulance. They'll probably be here before you get here. Meet me at the hospital."

"Which one you think you'll be at?" asked Khalid as the phone went silent. Moseley had already ended the call before he realized it.

I didn't know how I was going to get there, but wasn't going to bus hop from hospital to hospital looking for a Moseley Anderson.

"Calvin!" Khalid called out. "Calvin!"

Calvin turned down the volume of his stereo and yelled back, "What?"

"We gotta go to the hospital. Moseley got shot," I informed him, trying to remain calm about the incident, but deep down he was panicking.

"You don't have no other ride?" Calvin asked. "Hold up, is the nigga dead?"

"Nah, he said he's gon'na be okay. But I'm tryna meet him at the hospital."

"Which one?" Calvin asked.

"He doesn't know." I answered shrugging my shoulders.

"So what do you expect me to do? Drive around from hospital to hospital looking for Mo?" Calvin asked with an attitude rising in his voice. "I don't have gas anyway."

"You know what, man? I don't believe that, but it's cool," I replied as I picked up the phone and proceeded to dial Kiani's number.

"Hey," she picked up on the first ring.

"I need a huge favor."

"What are you going to give me in return?" she said in a low and seductive voice.

"No, Kiani. All sex aside, my boy just got shot and I need to get to the hospital."

"Well, what hospital is he at?" Kiani asked.

"I don't know yet. That's the only thing," I answered.

"All right, then I guess we have some searching to do," Kiani answered. "Give me your address. I'm on the way."

Damn, I thought, a feeling of relief coming over me. *This girl is my angel.*

Chapter Nine

Nyrique

"You know what, boy? Sometimes I ask myself how the fuck did I end up with you?" Shay said. She was in a heated argument with her boyfriend, Nyrique. He had come to San Bernardino from Los Angeles to visit her. The trip was sudden, but Nyrique was determined to come regardless of Shay's permission.

Dior was in the kitchen of the dorm, hearing every loud word that came out of Nyrique's and Shay's mouth. She did her best to tune them out by engaging herself in a news article for her journalism class, but couldn't keep one ear from listening in.

"Who the hell do you think you are? You can't just come up to my dorm and raid my room!" Shay said as she picked up her clothes on the floor. "And you need to apologize to Dior because she didn't do anything to you and you got her clothes thrown all over the place!"

"Fuck that. I didn't know they were hers," Nyrique responded.

"Why are you here?"

"What do you mean?"

Shay gave him a stern look. "Nyrique, please. You never show up unannounced on a weekend. I didn't invite you," she said.

Nyrique walked toward her and said, "Why? You were expecting someone else? You invited that nigga Khalid?"

Shay rolled her eyes angrily. She was annoyed with the man she had been seeing on and off for the past three years. Between his thug nature and many ladies to be suspicious of, the relationship was taking a turn for the worse.

"Yeah, I know he's out of jail. And he's trying to get with you. I saw his letter!" Nyrique shouted.

"He's not trying to get with me! And how did you know he wrote me a letter?" Shay asked, her arms folded across her chest and attitude written all over her face.

"You certainly didn't tell me," Nyrique snapped. "I stopped by your house."

"And my mother let you in?"

"Yeah, I went in your room and saw the letter in your dresser drawer. Why in the hell didn't you tell me he was writing you?" Nyrique asked, moving in on Shay.

"It wasn't none of your business, first of all."

"Wasn't none of my business? Shay, he was writing you and you are my damn business!" Nyrique said, angrier than before.

"Well, anyway . . . no, I was not expecting Khalid. Don't try to make me look like the bad person because you feel stupid."

"Shay, you better not be playing me," Nyrqiue said calmly.

"Nyrique, I swear I am not cheating."

Nyrique sighed and felt calm enough to hug her tenderly. "So why are you talking to this blood behind my back?"

"I don't think he bang, baby," Shay lied. She led Nyrique to her bed and sat him down. Her hands massaged his shoulders and he threw his head back in relaxation.

"Yeah, he a blood. Seen that mu'fucka at Fairfax. We got into it with his ass at the Expo. I almost busted his ass wide open."

Shay rolled her eyes and snickered, "Yeah, I'm sure."

Nyrique turned around and playfully pinned her down to the bed. Her eyes grew wide and he released his grip. "Oh, so you don't believe me huh?"

"Nah, I believe you," Shay said, smiling. She leaned up and kissed him sensually. He drew back and stood up. "What's wrong?" she asked him.

Nyrique answered, "I love you, Shay. And I want to be with you. Hell, I wanna lock you down and take you out the city. Get you settled in the valley somewhere. Knock you up with my kids—"

"Um, wife me first!" Shay interjected.

"Oh yeah, yeah!" Nyrique corrected. "Wife you up, then knock you up." He chuckled. "But my point is, you my girl. And I like our relationship. I don't want to feel threatened."

"By who?"

"You know who."

"Khalid?"

"That's right." Shay frowned uneasily and listened to the rest of Nyrique's speech. He continued: "Now, I trust you. I know you're a good girlfriend. But I want you to watch these male friends of yours."

"You have nothing to worry about," Shay assured him. She felt partly bad about not coming clean with Nyrique about her past with Khalid. The truth was she did used to have a thing for Khalid prior to him getting locked up, and seeing him after his release had re-lit the flame. But she knew this couldn't be told to Nyrique. He'd lose his temper and throw a fit, something Shay had to avoid as long as possible.

"Oh, but I do. I saw the letter Khalid wrote you. It

seems to me like he has a lot of feelings for you. I trust you, it's him I don't trust."

Shay knew part of that was untrue. Obviously Nyrique didn't trust her enough. After all, he ran through her dorm room and ransacked her belongings. "If you trust me then why did you go through my clothes and stuff?"

Nyrique shook his head and chuckled. "Baby, I slip up too. Okay? It won't happen again." He stroked her cheek with his finger. She looked at him with her brown, dreamy eyes and made him fall in love all over again. "Now can I have some?" Nyrique asked with such silliness Shay thought he was kidding. But by the way he tugged on her belt she knew he was just anxious.

With that being understood, Shay and Nyrique made passionate love that she had gotten less of since moving away for college.

First Nyrique teased parts of her body with his ferocious tongue, making her squeal with passion. She grabbed his face and pulled it up to hers. She whispered for him to put it in. Nyrique did as told, but not before turning on the stereo for background noise. As long as he could hear the sensuous moans made by Shay, he was just fine.

Nyrique made her spread-eagle on her bed and whipped out his gift. He slowly inched in as if it were her first time again. He made a rhythmic movement in and out of her. Just knowing he was the only man to enjoy her sexually excited him and kept him hard for hours. Shay looked into the eyes of the only man she had ever been with intimately and felt a sense of comfort and belonging.

Aroused, the two went at it in a way they had not before. They looked into each other's eyes, held hands and the kissing almost never stopped. Neither would they until they both came in unison.

Chapter Ten

Kiani

We anxiously waited for a status report from the doctors working on Moseley. Kiani was resting peacefully in my lap and Anthony was texting one of his ladies on his cell phone. I couldn't fall asleep thanks to my mind wandering about the drama with Moseley. I needed to know what state he was in, and if the bullet wound did more damage than what we knew of.

"You gon' be all right, Khalid?" Anthony asked, taking a moment away from his BlackBerry. "You look like a wreck."

"I am," I confirmed. "Moseley getting shot? For some reason I feel like I had something to do with this."

Anthony's face frowned up and he asked me, "I've got to hear this. How do you feel like Moseley getting shot is your fault?"

I ran my fingers through Kiani's hair, her head still resting in my lap as if she felt nothing. I turned my attention toward Anthony and answered, "You know, I never forgave myself for becoming a gangbanger. I see that had somewhat of an influence on Moseley. He would've never been shot, let alone in this situation, had he not become a gang-banger."

"So you think Moseley started banging because of you?" Anthony asked me.

I shrugged my shoulders and answered, "Well, I certainly wasn't the best influence back in the day. Where you think he got the idea of it being okay to be a blood? Not from that Bible he was reading. Not from his mother or father."

Anthony nodded his head, understanding the point I was making. "I feel you, but you can't hold yourself responsible for other's actions. You were locked up; that could've been Moseley's wake-up call. He didn't get the message and still wanted to get put on 20s. Don't blame yourself. It wasn't your fault, Khalid," he said with compassion.

Deep down, I knew Anthony was right. I wasn't the sole reason Moseley joined a gang, but I definitely felt I was an influence. For that, I'd never be able to forgive myself.

We waited another grueling hour, and the sound of the waiting room door opening was a relief. A tall doctor came into the room, dressed in a white lab coat over his green scrubs. He looked down at his clipboard and scribbled something down.

"Excuse me," the doctor said in a monotone voice.

At the sound of the doctor in the room, I shook Kiani out of her slumber and stood up. As I walked over to the doctor he put the clipboard in his left arm and shook my hand with his right. "Well, the good news is Moseley is going to be just fine. He lost a huge amount of blood so we need to keep him a couple more days to monitor his health."

I nodded my head and said, "That's fine. We'll visit him everyday."

"Would you all like to see him now?" asked the six-foot doctor.

I nodded my head anxiously and beckoned Kiani and Anthony over to us.

The doctor continued, "He's hooked up to the IV and the anesthesia might make him a little drowsy and woozy. The nurse will show you to the room." He flashed a smile and left us with the nurse.

We followed the nurse to the room in the California Hospital. The smell of the hospital was familiar, being that I had visited a hospital many times to visit wounded fellow gang members after they had been stabbed or shot. Moseley was in the last room at the end of the long hallway. After informing us of the thirty-minute time limit, the nurse let us have our moment alone.

"What up Moseley?" I asked, feeling relieved that he was okay. His eyes were half opened and he looked drained, but other than that, my boy was alive and well.

"What's good, blood?" he asked in response.

I wanted to tell him to cut all the blood shit out because that's what got him in the hospital in the first place. "How you feelin'?" I decided to ask him instead.

Moseley replied slowly, "I feel like getting revenge on some crabs when I get up out of here. That shit ain't cool, you know?"

Clueless to just about everything, Kiani asked, "What happened?"

"I thought I told you," I quickly butted in. I knew I gave vague details to her, but for a good reason. I didn't feel Kiani should involve herself in these matters.

"Moseley," she said to him, though looking me dead in my eyes.

"I got shot by some 30s crips at King Park today," Moseley informed without waiting to hear my objection to him informing Kiani about his brush with death.

"My cousin is a crip from there. I could find out who was at the park," Kiani volunteered wholeheartedly. "We can have them in jail, where they belong."

"Kiani!" I yelled. Had Kiani been a bit more street-smart, she would've known that Moseley was not hoping to find these crips to inform the police. Moseley had other intentions, cruel intentions.

She jumped at the anger in my tone. "What's the problem?" she asked me. "Don't you want these boys to pay for what they did?"

"Oh, hell yeah! Do that, sweetheart. What's your name? Kiana . . . Kiani?" Moseley egged her on, hopping she could play a key role in his revenge process.

"No," I rejected. "Don't do a god damn thing. Kiani, this doesn't concern you. Moseley, if you want to get back at them niggas, then do it on your own terms. Find 'em yourself."

"What's your fuckin' problem?" Moseley asked.

"Don't volunteer to do things that can get you fucked up!" I yelled at Kiani.

"By who? Certainly not you!" she said, showing another side of her that I had never seen before. There was a little fire in the Baldwin Hills beauty.

"Hell, nah, not by me! Suppose word get out that you gave Moseley the names of those niggas. And if those same niggas get shot and killed, of course shit is gon' lead to you and Moseley's stupid ass!" I said, hoping I was making reasonable sense.

"Why I got to be stupid?" Moseley asked with a chuckle, whacked out from the anesthesia as the doctor had warned.

I answered, "Because that's the kind of move you're making if you go back and hit them crips up!"

"Oh yeah, you know all about being stupid and making

mistakes, don't you?" Moseley said with sarcasm. "Spent a couple of years in jail for it, huh?"

There was silence. I was tired of the low blows coming from what were supposed to be my supportive friends. I held my tongue in the past, but now I was going to give Moseley a piece of my mind. Not only had he hit me with a low-blow comment, but had the nerve to put me out there in front of Kiani. I tapped Kiani's shoulder and requested that she leave. I didn't want her to hear what I had to say to Moseley, so she willingly left at my request.

"Now look Moseley or Mo, whatever the fuck you wanna go by," I said once Kiani was out of the room. "I'm gon'na forget you said that last comment 'cuz your brain is fucked up from a loss of blood right now. If you wanna hit them niggas up then do it. But I don't want any part in it, and I don't want her ass involved. You heard dat, mu'-fucka?" I headed toward the door.

Moseley adjusted himself in the reclining hospital bed. He grimaced from the pain he still felt in his arm. "What's the problem? Nobody's gon'na find out," Moseley said.

"Yeah, the cops say that same bullshit to informants. Next thing you know they dead," I said. "I'm just taking the safe way out and that's for neither of us to get involved."

"Khalid, you blocking me from handling my business," Moseley told me.

"Exactly, *your* business. This doesn't have shit to do with me or Kiani," I said, heading for the door. Before leaving I reminded him, "Keep her out of it."

"Hey, Hide!" Moseley called out, deciding to call me by my hood name. "She's just a bitch! They come a dime a dozen, remember?"

I looked at him and thanked God he had been through enough pain because if he hadn't, I would've fucked his ass up for another slick comment. I switched glances with Anthony, who pretended to be oblivious to me and Moseley's conversation.

"Ant, I'll see you at the crib," I said, ignoring Moseley's comment because in my heart I knew Kiani was so much more than that.

Chapter Eleven

Anthony

I had Kiani drop me off at the house after leaving the hospital. I made her promise me she would not get involved in Moseley's mess. I needed to know that she would keep her nose clean, and out of his mess. She'd only known him for a short time, and hopefully that was enough for her to convince her not get involved.

"Do you really care what I do?" she asked before I stepped out of the car.

I nodded my head and said, "Yes, I care about what you do . . . and I care about you. I'll call you tomorrow."

"I don't work so if you want to hang out . . . go job hunting again . . . go to the park," she suggested.

"Do I have to sneak into your crib?" I asked.

Kiani shrugged and said, "Well, I can come over here."

"Yeah, but I'm sure your parents are gon'na want to know who you're with. You probably got them goody two-shoes-parents who don't wanna see their little girl with a thug."

"I don't think you're a thug."

"But your peeps would."

"Do you think you're a thug?"

"Not anymore. But the older generation thinks all young, black males are thugs. Are your parents in that category?" I asked. I knew I wasn't a thug because I had already made up in my mind and heart that I was done gangbanging. But that wasn't going to be enough to convince others that I was through, especially the older generation that was so fixed on stereotyping the new generation. I would have to prove it with my actions, and so far I had no job and hadn't enrolled at a community college.

"Khalid—" She was overcome with guilt. We'd been seeing each other for a month and I hadn't been introduced to her parents. At this point, introducing me to her folks would say a lot about how she felt about me. I knew Kiani was still scared to bring me home to Mom and Dad, something a girl should be proud to do. I wouldn't consider us official until she made that move.

I shushed her and said, "How about you work on introducing me to your parents. Then we'll take it from there."

A look of shock came over her face and she told me to get out. I apologized if I offended her as I stepped out of the car. Her increasing anger was made official when she sped off after I closed the door.

Maybe I shouldn't have said that, I thought, thinking about my last words to her. *Then we'll take it from there? What was I thinking?* I shook my head disapprovingly, upset with myself for not choosing a better choice of words. If I was going to be with Kiani, I would definitely need to think before speaking . . . especially when it came to matters that were important to me.

I walked off and went into the house. Calvin wasn't here, but Anthony was. He was cleaning his shoes with a toothbrush and shoe cleaner as he did at the end of every day. It was his mission to stay fresh from head to toe. Part of accomplishing that mission was to keep a clean pair of shoes.

He stopped brushing the side of his Nike blazers and said, "Hey Khalid.What's up?"

"What up, Ant?" I asked. I proceeded to go into the bathroom.

"Hold up!" called Anthony. "C'mere for a minute. I gotta talk to you."

Frustrated, I walked over to the couch where he was sitting. I expected this to be about what happened in the hospital between Moseley and me. "What about?"

"Moseley." Go figure.

"Man, if this is about the incident in the hospital, you can forget it! I meant what I said," I began.

"Nah, I just want to be the unifier. I don't want two of my boys walking around mad at each other over some avoidable bullshit."

"I'm over it now. I said what I had to say about his problem."

"I talked to Moseley after you left," Anthony informed.

"Really now? What about?" I asked sarcastically.

Anthony smiled and replied, "You know we talked about you, Khalid. He said he was glad you were back and wanted things to be like old times."

"That'll never happen. I'm a changed person," I cut in. "I don't wanna be bangin' on the streets no more and I don't want to be affiliated with anyone that is."

Anthony continued as if I never interrupted him. "Moseley said he used to look up to you in high school. He wanted the same respect you got, and wanted to be gansta just like Hide! It's funny because he really expects you to be down with him."

"Anthony, I can't mess myself up. I'm trying to do shit right. I don't have time to be gang-banging!" I exclaimed. "You know they got me on this three-strikes-and-I'm-out bull shit. I fucked up three times already, but the first time I messed up I was young so I caught a break. I should be rotting in jail for the rest of my life right now. Slanging crack cocaine, assault with a deadly weapon and armed robbery! I'm way past due. Any little thing I get caught for means a lot of time in jail. I don't want to be what the streets are trying to make me, Anthony. Shit, what's so hard about that? Getting back into that gangbanging shit ain't gon' do nothing but fuck me up."

"Well, what the fuck were you reading in jail? Books by Tookie Williams?" Anthony joked.

His joke fell flat with me. "I'm serious."

Anthony sighed. He ran the bristles of the brush across his shos. He was at a loss for words due to my seriousness. I guess he didn't know how to approach the reformed me.

Once he found the words, he continued on with his original point, to tell me what was going on in Moseley's head. "Well, Moseley thinks you're just frontin for Kiani or whoever. And according to him, ain't no future in yo' frontin'. He also told me to tell you that men don't choose females over their niggas."

"This ain't about Kiani," I clarified.

"Mosley has a point," Anthony said.

"What! So you agree with him?" I asked angrily. It would be wise for Anthony to remain neutral, and not even give off the slightest idea of siding with Moseley.

"I don't fully agree with him," Anthony objected. "I'm just saying he has a point. You are supposed to be Moseley's homie. You're supposed to have people's back, at least the ones you care for."

"Even if that means risking *my* freedom and jeopardizing *my* life?" I asked.

Anthony looked at me like I was on crack. He was obviously confused. "What do you mean?"

I pounded my fist into the other open hand. I explained to him my situation and my problem as best as I could. "Man, it ain't no secret. Mu'fuckas know me on these streets and as much as I try to fight it, some of 'em want me back in jail. I'm tryna do better with my life and it ain't gon'na be easy. I'm already in violation with the boys from Van Ness Gangsters, I have cops who will do anything so much as to framing me to get me back in jail, and now I got my friends on my head because I can't take up for them how they want me to. I can't help Moseley pop them crips off 'cuz if I'm linked to it my ass is gon'! You think I'm tryna go back? Hell nah! I'm gon'na keep outta jail, keep outta trouble, keep a low profile and not let anybody screw me up . . . even if it means pissing my boys off."

Anthony shook his head. He had nothing to say because he knew I was right. Why should I risk my future for someone else? There was no arguing that.

"Damn, I feel you, man. I mean, not like that because I've never been to jail . . . but you know what I mean. That's some real shit. What happened to you, man?"

"What do you mean, what happened to me?" I asked as I started walking toward the kitchen.

"You changed . . . a lot," Anthony said as if it was his first time realizing it.

I shrugged and said, "I woke up. That's what I did. I woke up."

"Well, you're changing. And it's scaring everybody," Anthony admitted.

"That's funny . . . 'cuz I was thinking the same thing about some of my friends."

I didn't realize it until Anthony brought it up. I was changing, like my friends. But the difference was that I was changing for the good. I was glad Anthony was giving me a heads-up about the opinions of others on the new me. But that didn't mean I would return to the old Khalid: young, black, and don't give a fuck. That had gotten me in enough trouble.

Chapter Twelve

Calvin

The fixed, cold stare in his eyes couldn't be taken as penetrating. It was deadening, and Dior felt that if looks could kill she would be dead. Calvin gave her a look that expressed his anger and frustration.

"I don't get it! No matter how may fucking times we go over this, you always manage to screw up. I could slap the taste out of your mouth!" Calvin stormed.

"Don't threaten me, Calvin. What was I supposed to do? Not accept the gift?" Dior asked.

"Exactly, stupid ass!"

"Don't call me stupid!" Dior cried. Tears began flowing down her face. She pushed him with all her might, but he didn't budge. Even her anger and fury wasn't enough to move him.

"Well, stop acting like it," Calvin said, grabbing her arm and squeezing it tightly and harshly.

"Ow! Stop!" Dior screamed. "Khalid!"

At the sound of my name, I ran in the room and hoped Calvin wasn't putting his hand on her. If he was, I was gon'na piss another one of my friends off. "What's going on?" I asked, catching Calvin releasing his grip on Dior.

"Nothing, blood. Just mind your business," Calvin said.

"Don't hit her Calvin," I told him. "It ain't worth all that."

"Don't tell me what to do with my bitch!"

Dior gasped. "Calvin!" She looked embarrassed. She looked at me to watch for a facial expression relating to Calvin's last comment. Nothing. "Thanks, but it's cool."

I nodded my head with assurance. "All right, holla if you need me." I rubbed her shoulder.

"I will," she said.

Just as I turned and walked out of the door, Calvin slammed it shut. I stood nearby just in case. I could hear every word of their argument.

"Oh, you will?" Calvin asked, mocking her cruelly. "You want to be with Khalid?"

"No, Calvin! Hell no!" Dior said as she wiped her eyes.

"Then stop inviting him into our relationship. First you loaning that nigga money and now you need his help. You on some bullshit!" Calvin said. He was enraged.

Nothing Dior did or said could better the situation. "Calvin, you're pissed off at something else and you're taking it out on me!" she yelled. "You know I hate that shit!"

"No, I'm pissed off at you. You get some bracelet from a male friend of yours and got the balls to wear it to my crib!"

Dior shook her head. "Baby, I'm so sorry! It was a gift! It was just an old gift given to me a long time ago!"

"So why are you acting all scared if you know you were wrong in the first place?" Calvin didn't receive an answer. "Are you deaf, girl?"

Dior shook her head.

"Mute?"

She shook her head again.

"Then speak!"

"You're scaring me," said Dior. She never knew it would get this bad with him. If she knew Calvin would have tripped this bad, she would have left the Guess? charm bracelet her ex-boyfriend Terry purchased for her at her dorm. She decided to wear it out of mere fashion choice. It matched the other jewelry she was wearing. As soon as Calvin saw the unknown piece of jewelry, he asked her. Opposed to lying, Dior told him where it came from. Jealousy immediately boiled inside of Calvin.

"Damn, if you wanted a bracelet you shoulda told me!" He laughed deliriously.

Dior shrugged. "He gave it to me when we were together. I never asked for it."

"I think you're lying."

"I think you're crazy."

Calvin, out of nowhere, grabbed Dior's face abruptly. His rough, strong hand cupped her jaw. "You think I'm crazy now? Let me find out you're fucking around on me—I'll show you crazy."

If Dior hated anything about Calvin, it was his threats. More than that, she hated the fact that he would actually go through with them. She held back the tears in her watery eyes as Calvin released his grip on her face. She didn't know where these abrupt changes in their relationship came from. One day they were on top of the clouds, the next they were falling down a bottomless pit of insecurity and miscommunication; two things that threatened to ruin their relationship.

"I'm not cheating on you," she reassured him once more.

Calvin nodded, even though in his heart he was skeptical.

"Now that pussy is mine, right?" Calvin asked as his hands palmed her ass.

Dior nodded bashfully and said, "Yes, it is."

"All right then, get it ready for Daddy 'cuz we're going out tonight," Calvin said. He turned her around and slapped both cheeks of her ass. "I'm going to get the car washed so be ready when I get back."

Dior gathered her pride and headed toward the bathroom with some clothes she kept over the house and a bath towel.

I quickly moved from the door and sat in the kitchen.

"Dior, Dior, Dior," I sighed as I looked down at the magazine in my hands. A few seconds later, I felt someone standing over me. I looked up and saw Calvin looking at me. I stood up, got on his level and shrugged my shoulders. "What the fuck?"

Calvin quickly looked at me up and down. "So you and Dior are the best of friends now?"

"Fall back, Calvin. What do you mean by that?" I asked.

"When she calls, you come running!"

"She called my name!"

"Yeah, so?"

"If you were to hurt her, I was gon'na have to hurt you."

"Nigga, what I do with my bitch is between me and her."

"But you ain't gon' hurt her."

"And you should mind your business from now on. You don't have to worry about us."

"And you don't have to worry about us, either." I said

"Us who?" Calvin asked.

"Me and Dior," I answered. "You got yours, and I got mine."

Calvin nodded his head slowly, turned around and walked out the front door. I sat back down, and began pondering just how true my short-tempered friend was.

Chapter Thirteen

Dior

Dior hurled vomit into the toilet bowl of her dorm bathroom. She coughed and hung her head low from the pain she was feeling. Shay rushed into the bathroom and aided her friend. She held a towel around Dior's neck, wiped her sweaty forehead, and soothed her. "It's okay, Dior. It's okay. Why are you crying?"

Dior shook her head. She said, "Shay, it's not okay. I know why I'm sick."

"You got food poisoning, right?" Shay asked, believing the original answer Dior gave her earlier in the day.

"Nah," Dior sobbed. "It's not that, Shay."

Shay sighed and looked up in the air, the answer coming to her with no guessing involved. "You're pregnant."

Dior looked away shamefully, flushed the toilet, and rose to her feet. She looked in the mirror and grabbed her face towel. She washed away the remains of vomit on the corners of her mouth and rinsed out her mouth with water.

"Damn, Dior. That was your pregnancy test in the trash can?" asked a surprised Shay.

"Whose else would it be?"

"I thought it was Natalie's or Cara's," Shay said. She really did wish it belonged to their other roommates.

Dior wished it was too, but it wasn't. She was pregnant. She didn't know how far along, but she knew it was over a couple of weeks. She had slacked off on birth control and Calvin wasn't an advocate for condoms. Just thinking about the change of course in her life was making her cry.

"Oh shit, Shay! This is so wrong. Wrong! This isn't how it's supposed to be. I'm supposed to get married first, then have kids. I'm too young to get pregnant!" Dior exclaimed.

Shay tried to calm her friend down. "Slow down, Dior. Look, we're going to the clinic right away!"

"Oh my goodness," said a hysterical Dior. She got up and ran to her room. Shay followed her out, demanding to know what else was wrong.

Dior was laid out on the bed and shook her head uncontrollably. "What about school? What am I going to do about school? I'll have to drop out!"

"No, no, no!" Shay refused, not wanting to complete her sophomore year without her friend. "No! You're not dropping out. We'll do whatever we have to do."

"I can't believe I'm pregnant," Dior said. "I should have kept up with birth control."

"Why'd you start slipping?"

"Girl, it started off with missing one day, then a couple days, then a week, then weeks—"

"—And pretty soon you just stopped altogether," Shay finished her friend's sentence.

"Mmm-hmm." Dior sighed, feeling defeated and stressed-out.

"You and Calvin were having unprotected sex all along?"

"Mmm-hmm."

"Dior, how did you expect not to get pregnant?"

"Having unprotected sex doesn't mean you'll get pregnant," Dior said, dumfounded.

"In your case it does!" Shay replied. "Having unprotected sex only increased your chances of getting pregnant. You should have known better."

"I know, Shay. It was a mistake."

"Are you going to get an abortion?" Shay asked.

"I can't!"

"What do you mean you can't?"

Dior answered, "Well, I'll consider it, but in my heart I don't want to."

Shay looked in the direction toward the door where their two roommates, Natalie and Cara, were standing.

"Is everything okay, ladies?" Natalie asked.

"Yes, we're good. She's just really sick. That's all," Shay answered.

Even Natalie and Cara knew that wasn't true. But neither would ask about what was really wrong. They each had a class to get to, so no need to stick around when all the data wasn't being told to them.

"Well, we're off to class. See you when we get back," Cara replied.

They waved good-bye and left Shay and Dior in privacy. Shay grabbed Dior's cell phone and dialed Calvin's number.

"What are you doing?" Dior asked.

"Calling Calvin," Shay answered.

"No!" Dior yelled, frighten.

"Why?" Shay asked as the phone rang, awaiting an answer.

"He'll make me get an abortion. No, please don't tell him!" Dior pleaded.

Calvin answered the phone. "Hello, Dior?"

"No, it's me, Shay. Calvin, I was calling you because I wanted to know if you had talked to Dior at all today."

"Not today. Why?"

"Because I haven't seen her and her cell is here. You know what? She might have went up to the food court to get a bite to eat and just left her phone," Shay said, thinking on her feet.

"All right, well, tell her to call me when you see her, please," Calvin requested.

"Okay, bye."

Dior found the strength to hug her best friend. "Ooh, thank you! Thank you!"

"Don't thank me, Dior. We're going to the doctor as soon as possible!" Shay insisted.

"Okay. I'll schedule an appointment right away," Dior replied. "But for now, this is between me and you."

"Well, when are you going to tell Calvin that you're pregnant?" Shay asked as she rose to her feet. She walked to the mirror mounted on the wall and let her hair fall from the bun on top of her head. Through the mirror she saw Dior shrug. "How far along do you think you are?"

"I gotta be about a month at the most. I just stopped birth control last month," she answered.

"Damn it girl," Shay said. "You in some shit now."

"I know it," Dior agreed. "Some deep shit."

Chapter Fourteen

Shay

The doorbell chimed, waking me out of a staring contest with the television. I rose to my feet and saw who was at the front door. To my surprise, it was Shay, down in the City of Angels for the weekend. Her visits had been rare to none since returning to college. However, Dior found time to make it down here every weekend to see her man. I wished Shay could have put forth the same effort. But I was more than glad to see her this day, being that I hadn't seen her in a month.

"What's up, stranger?"

"I'm no stranger. You are. You're the one who's been locked up for the past three years," Shay said, entering the house.

"More jail jokes, huh?" I asked, closing the front door and locking it.

"And that's just what they are . . . jokes. I don't mean it. Give me a hug," Shay said as she grabbed me.

We hugged. I inhaled the fragrance she wore. She was wearing the sweet pea fragrance from Bath & Body Works. I know that scent from anywhere.

"So, where have you been?" I asked. I sat down on the couch, turned the television off, and gave her my undivided attention. I tried my best not to get distracted by her beauty and all the sexual thoughts that came to mind (hey, I'm a man) as she blabbed about school and work. Her long, brown, thick hair was pulled into a ponytail. I loved her hair in ponytails because it brought out her face. Her eyes, though sparkling, had a certain sadness to them that I wanted to discover. "Can I cut you off for a minute?"

"Umm . . . okay," She allowed. "Why?"

"You are so beautiful." I leaned against the arm of the couch, my face resting on top of my fist as I admired her.

She immediately blushed and smiled bashfully as her face shifted downward and hid emotion. "Khalid—"

"No, you really are. What the hell are you doing with that crip Nyrique? He doesn't know how to handle you." I don't know why I decided to bring Nyrique into what could've been a innocent conversation about her, but it would prove to be a fatal mistake.

"Oh—and you do?" Shay asked angrily.

I had said the wrong thing at the right time. I saw her emotions change from flattered to pissed in a matter of seconds. Shay had revealed a glimpse of the girl I knew before being hauled off to jail. Now she was conforming to the defensive diva that had just recently came about. "Shay, I didn't mean it like that."

"But you said it like that and I took it like that," Shay flared. She rose to her feet and, pointing her finger in my face, she continued, "And that's another thing I want to talk to you about. Nyrique."

"And how he can't do for you?"

"And I suppose you can do for me? Khalid, you don't know shit about my relationship!"

"I know enough to see you ain't as happy as you should be." I knew that the more this battle went on, the more armor we would lose and our true feelings could be revealed.

Shay laughed hysterically. "Oh and what? No, let me guess . . . you are the one who can make me happy."

"I can give you what you need," I said, lowering my tone with each word.

Shay stood akimbo, looked at me with those sad, dreamy eyes and shook her head. "What I don't need is a headache and that's the only thing you're giving me."

"I can give you some Tylenol," I chuckled. My efforts to lighten and ease the conversation were pointless. Shay did not even crack a smile. Uneasily, I returned to the gist of our conversation. "You wanted to talk about Nyrique?" That was the last thing I wanted to talk about, but it was what she wanted. Therefore, I'd let her say what it was she had to say.

"Yeah, I do. I'm going to be brief. The last time Nyrique and I talked, which was yesterday, you came up," she began.

"Go figure," I rudely interrupted.

"Khalid!" she whined. I apologized for thinking out loud. She continued, "He sees you as a threat to our relationship. He asked me not to speak to you."

"And are you telling me that's what you're going to do?"

Shay shook her head and responded, "No, just listen. I'm not just going to stop talking to you as a friend because that wouldn't be nice of me. I'm just going to respect his wishes and tone down on us a little bit."

"So you're not going to talk me," I bluntly spat.

She was confused. "Khalid, what do you mean?" she asked.

"You only speak to me a little bit to begin with. So what the fuck do you mean you're going to tone it down? Might as well not speak at all . . . don't speak to me ever! Respect your man's wishes!" I yelled angrily. Though we had a rocky and confusing friendship, I still considered Shay a good friend, and I wouldn't cut her off for anyone.

Shay looked at me coldly. "Boy, please! I have my reasons as to why we don't talk as much anymore. I am busy tryna' stay in college so I can better myself as a person and better my life! Excuse me for wanting success!"

"That's a bullshit excuse and you know it. You sure find time to talk to Nyrique," I replied.

"Well, unlike you, Nyrique is my boyfriend! We're in a relationship."

"Yeah, a relationship! And I'm the threat. You're so dumb that you can't even see that he's the threat to our relationship. He's ruining our friendship, Shay. Don't look at me like you don't know. He's the one who doesn't want you talking to me! I'm just surprised that you're going to do what he's asking. Somebody actually tamed your ass."

Had the sound of the doorbell not interrupted me, Shay would have been in tears after hearing what I had to say. Thank God the doorbell rang, but I knew it was the evil work of the devil when I saw Kiani on the porch. I paused for a minute and wondered how the hell I was going to work this one out.

"Well," Kiani asked after getting tired of waiting on the porch. "Are you going to let me in?"

Without muttering any words, I opened the door and let her in. Before seeing Shay, she grabbed me and kissed me as if we were an official couple. I was so stunned by her kiss I didn't even have time to pull back.

"Hey baby," Kiani said, patting my chest. "How have you been?"

All of a sudden, I was mute and deaf, only hearing the thoughts in my head. Kiani and Shay were both in my presence—two women that I cared for in completely opposite ways. One of them didn't care for me half as much as I cared for her and the other cared for me more than I cared for her, which was overbearing but appealing.

"Hi, I'm Kiani, Khalid's girlfriend," Kiani said, walking toward Shay with an extended arm.

Shay shook her hand and introduced herself. "And I'm Shay, an old friend of Khalid's. I came by to see if Moseley was out of the hospital and ran into him."

"Oh well, don't mind me. I have to tinkle. Khalid, where is your bathroom? Excuse me." She excused herself and I pointed to the bathroom down the hall.

Shay and I were in another awkward moment of silence. Shay waited until she heard the sound of the bathroom door close, then shattered the stillness in the room. She said, "Tinkle? You got yourself a class act."

"Don't start."

"Oh no, Mr. Khalid, I am going to start. I didn't know you had a girlfriend."

"Me either."

"What?"

"I never officially asked her out."

"What *did* you do? You just initiated her into your heart with some dick?"

"Shay."

"And you had the nerve to try to ask me about Nyrique! Getting on my relationship and you're in one of your own."

"It's not what you think."

"Well, she thinks it and so do I. You can tamper with her heart. You might break it if you're lucky, but not mine."

"Yeah, I'll leave that for Nyrique."

"Fuck you." Shay left immediately.

Kiani had snuck up behind me. I hoped she hadn't heard what just went down.

"Well, what are we?" Kiani sadly asked. Her heart was shattered, I knew it.

I felt extremely low and answered, "It's something I want, I know that for sure. At first I didn't consider it serious."

"Just sex."

"Yeah, but at the end of that day you got me and I've been trying to fight it."

"Why? Don't you care about me?"

"I wasn't ready to jump into commitment, at least not with you. But honestly, I felt like you pushed me."

"You weren't ready to jump into it, but I pushed you." She held her head down low, searching for the words to say. Kiani looked up at me with watery eyes, but no tears falling. "So now what?"

"I'm jumping."

Chapter Fifteen

Kiani

Soon after confessing that I was ready to be with Kiani, I noticed she wasn't one to hold back from me. I thought that would be her initial reaction after hearing me say she pushed me into this, but she remained the same. Caring, sweet, and innocent.

In fact, my attitude came to a conversion. With every passing day, I grew closer to her and wanted to know more about her. I was attached now, by the heart, and for the first time in a long time I was feeling passionate about love.

Weeks went by and our relationship grew to be blissful. I would say we had some similarities with Calvin and Dior, the designer couple. Speaking of those two, things between them were getting extremely rocky. Dior hadn't been to the house in two weeks and Calvin was aggravated by every little thing. Eventually I would find out the key to their madness, but right now I had my focus on Kiani.

My focus on Kiani was so powerful that Shay was placed on the back burner. We had not spoken since our last argument . . . three months ago. She was obeying the relationship rules of Nyrique while I dedicated myself to falling in love with Kiani.

At this stage in our relationship, I wouldn't say I was in love with Kiani yet. I had much love for her, however. Kiani could walk into a room with an enlightening smile and make my day. She was undoubtedly the joy I needed in my life, which was a ball of confusion.

Kiani was my rock, my bridge, and my angel. She got me a job at her father's warehouse. She had introduced me to him days prior. I put my good-boy act on and worked the charm. Her mom adored me and dad favored me. Now I had a job at his warehouse, getting paid nine dollars an hour.

Even though it was my first week, I managed to show ambition and good labor. I followed every order given, completed any task asked to perform, and listened to every rule and command. Kiani's father even mentioned after my third day that with the way I was working, I'd get a promotion in no time.

It warmed me to receive such a compliment. I was so use to hearing jail facilitators and policemen say I was no good and born to rot in jail. But it was Kiani and her family that helped me recognize that I was better than that.

Getting in good with her parents was no walk in the park. I had to work my way in there. Kiani's father, Mr. Wesley, was obviously overprotective of his daughter and wanted to know who the young man that had her daughter's heart was. He was going to dig in deep to get it. The conversation Mr. Wesley and I had when we first met was a man-to-man talk that I would remember for the rest of my life.

"Young man, tell me about yourself," he said in a powerful voice.

"Well, what would you like to know?" I asked him, trying to sound just as powerful.

"Tell me about your family, your past, and your goals."
He was straightforward.

"Well, my family? My mother and father aren't really . . .
my mom—well, my dad,—" I hesitated. I had two choices.
I could bullshit my way through this or tell Mr. Wesley the
truth, flaws and all, and hope he could take me for who I
was. "My mom and dad weren't involved in my life. I don't
know where they are now. For all I know they could be
dead. I lost contact with them when I went to jail three
years ago."

Mr. Wesley, caught off guard by my honesty about going
to jail, cleared his throat and loosened the tie around his
neck. "Why were you in jail, young man?" he asked, bringing his left ankle to his right knee. He sat back, raised his
glasses over the brim of his nose, and folded his arms across
his chest.

"Armed robbery."

"And you served three years?"

"Three years of a seven-year sentence. I was a juvenile
and I had good behavior in jail."

Mr. Wesley nodded, but it seemed disapproving. I was
certain that he didn't want me with his daughter. "Was that
your first time going to jail?"

"Th—third . . . time," I hesitated. He could smell the
fear within. I always got nervous when people, especially el-
ders, asked about my past. Just having them view me as a
criminal, even subhuman, was upsetting and sometimes unbearable. The judgment they make without knowing me as
a person belittled me because I knew I was more than the
thug I was some years ago. If Mr. Wesley could overlook
my past and see where I wanted my future to be then he
would see me as a suitable man for his daughter.

"The first two times were for what?" he asked with almost no emotion, disabling me to make a judgement on
him.

"The first time I was fourteen. I was caught with some illegal drugs and got a year in juvy. I had to take summer school to make up for eighth grade. Second time I got locked up, I was a freshman at Dorsey. I got into a huge fight with this crip and beat him up with a pistol. I got put in jail for a year—the charge was assault with a deadly weapon and possession of a firearm. I missed out on the end of freshman year and the beginning of my sophomore year. I made that up in summer school too. So when I got out, I enrolled at Fairfax, completed school and got locked up the summer I graduated."

Mr. Wesley was shocked, more so bewildered that I left no stone unturned. I told him what he wanted to know: the truth.

"Are you in a gang?"

"I use to bang," I chuckled, but it wasn't in a funny way. More regretful. "They used to call me Hide. But I dropped all that when I got out of jail. I left it alone, and I don't plan on going back."

"Why did you join in the first place? Why join a gang when you are going to want out years down the line?" Mr. Wesley loosened up, even changing his position in the chair. If he had a pen and paper in his hand, he would have looked like a reporter and this was his story that would make front-page news.

"When I joined a gang I was thinking a few years down the line. When I joined a gang, I felt like I was somebody, like I was good enough. I meant something to somebody and I was accepted after proving myself worthy. You know?"

"But why a gang? Why not a boys and girls club?"

As I warmed up to Mr. Wesley, he warmed up to me. The tone of his voice was now endearing, and I felt like he cared about me . . . genuinely.

"Gangs were all I knew, Mr. Wesley. I was surrounded by

it. The streets of LA raised me. Not my mom and dad. Not even the uncle I was sent to live with. Shoot, the streets raised them too."

Mr. Wesley stared at me and I saw some emotion. My eye for detail told me he was sympathetic toward me. He felt sorry for me. Little did he know, at times I felt sorry for myself.

"Young man," he began. "Many brothers get out of jail and say they are done with the streets. But I know the streets have a pretty strong hold on them. The streets call, and pretty soon they answer. How are you prepared to fight it?"

I shrugged and replied, "Well, I'm just going to have to put my energy into something else. I can't concern myself with the streets."

"It's going to hit close to home, Khalid."

"Why do you say that?"

"Don't you still associate yourself with the young men who are involved in gang activity?"

The first person to come to mind was Moseley. Without uttering a word, I just nodded my head.

"That's going to be the problem. It happens all the time with our young men trying to turn their lives around. Your friends might try to get you to go back into that same thug lifestyle that could end up being your undoing," said Mr. Wesley.

"They already have," I answered.

What I didn't tell Mr. Wesley was that his daughter was being brought into the gangbanger lifestyle just by relation. Her knowing somebody that knew somebody that was a gangbanger gave her indirect affiliation.

"And why should I let you date my daughter?" he asked. There was the question I had a ready, truthful answer prepared for.

"Because I'm a young man who can admit his faults, and

learn from them. I didn't come in here fronting for you. I am what I am, straight up. Kiani accepts that, and I hope you and your wife can do the same. The difference between me and those knuckleheads in the streets is that I am smart enough to get out off the streets," I answered.

Mr. Wesley nodded his head with approval. "You're a very smart young man. I want to do something for you. Now this is something I've never done before—especially for the guys Kiani has dated. But there's an employment opportunity at the warehouse I own. You can lift boxes and other large items, right?"

"Yeah, I can do that," I answered, nodding my head. If the job required physical strength, then I could get it done.

"Well, I'm willing to give you that job to help you get on your way. It pays nine dollars an hour—"

"I'll take it," I said excitingly, cutting him off.

My conversation with Mr. Wesley ended on a good note. He saw through my past and into the young man I had come to be. Things from there went uphill.

Even though my day shift ended at three o'clock, I clocked out around two-thirty to spend the rest of my day with Kiani. She was parked in front of the warehouse in her father's Porsche. I noticed her uplifting smile from far away. I got into the passenger seat and told her to take me out of here. After a long day's work, all I wanted to do was kick back, relax, and enjoy the evening with my girl.

"So I start my classes at LMU in two months, right . . ." Kiani paused.

"Yeah?" I asked, urging her on.

"Daddy thinks I should get an apartment in the area near there so I won't have to commute through traffic so much," Kiani said.

"Really?" Now she had my full attention. I opened my ears a little more to hear where she was going with this.

"Yes, really. And there's more. He even agrees that you can live with me!"

"Live with you?" I asked.

Part of me was happy as hell about living with her. That meant no more grouchy Calvin, no more spontaneity from Anthony, and no more nude Moseley. On the other side, I knew it was too soon to be moving in with each other. We had only known each other a little over six months, and just made ourselves a couple four months ago.

"Kiani, don't you think it's too soon to be moving in with each other?" I asked the question lingering on the mind of my opposing side.

"Well, if it's a little too much for you to handle, we can have separate bedrooms and his-and-her bathrooms," Kiani suggested.

"That sounds good, but it's a little more complicated than that," I stated. "Baby, it's a little too soon to be living together. Just keepin' it real."

Kiani sighed and asked, "Well, what would be an appropriate time for you, Khalid?"

"Maybe after a year or so."

"Oh, so you plan on keeping me around that long?"

She was joking, but for some reason I didn't find that funny. "Seriously, Kiani. Give me six more months."

"Six months?"

"Six months."

Kiani shrugged and made a left turn onto the main street. "They say you really get to know a person when you live with them."

"Well, let me get to know what I can first," I said.

That shouldn't have been too hard. With every day I was learning so much about her, about us, and about myself.

Chapter Sixteen

Moseley

There are only seven deadly sins. Lust, Gluttony, Greed, Sloth, Wrath, Envy and Pride. But one has been forgotten. There should actually be eight deadly sins. The eighth deadly sin: Revenge.

I believe it is a driving force in people that boils in their blood and makes them go mad. Some people go to their graves with revenge in their spirit. It's a sad thing. I vowed to myself that I would never let revenge consume me.

Moseley, on the other hand, had lost his mind bent on revenge. Every time we would converse, every other sentence was about him getting revenge on the crips that killed Jordan. One would think getting shot and almost having your life taken would be enough to transform. But no! Some brothas got to get shot a couple more times and thrown in jail more than once to get the bigger picture. I had been there, done that and did not wanna go back.

Moseley was now driven by revenge, and it was eating him up from the inside out. On many countless nights, he desperately called up any, and everybody he knew, looking for two kinds of people: Someone who had some kind of information on the 30s crip members involved in the shooting and someone who wanted in on the revenge.

Undoubtedly he found the second kind of people he was looking for. There were many bloods driven by revenge just by the principle. A blood getting knocked off by a crip is a means of justification. Moseley's fellow gang members were drawn into it just because they shared the same hood as Jordan. They found ways to tie themselves to the plan of revenge. The main associates were Nite, Slim, and Kush. Government names: James Knightly, Andrew Robinson, and Mohammed Walker. These were the forerunners of 20s bloods. If you were with them, you were automatically respected and credited.

Now that Moseley had his crew, he had to get his plan together. That became an every-other-day activity. But his daily routine was trying to get to Kiani, who he believed was a prime clue in this game. He was on her like white on rice. I had to keep a close watch on Moseley who would do just about anything to get close to a tip on who it was that shot him.

"I am sick to my stomach, nigga! I want to find out who they are so bad, I'd kill for it!" Moseley said to Calvin and Anthony.

They were all drinking their alcohol of choice, watching ESPN in the living room. Moseley was drinking Bombay gin straight from the clear bottle. Calvin was dressed in nothing but black khakis, sipping on malt liquor and drinking lightly because he had to work in a few hours.

"And I'm sick to my stomach of hearing you talk about it. Let it go and invest in some karma. What goes around comes around," Calvin said.

"Look who's talking!" Anthony laughed. "Moseley, you're only—" He paused and lowered his voice to a whisper. "Your only help is Kiani. She can talk to her cousin, remember?"

"What? Wait a minute! The girl Khalid is talking to is the one that can tell you who it was from 30s that shot Jordan?" Calvin asked, whispering just as quietly.

Moseley nodded. "She's on her way over here too."

"She and Khalid are going out?" Anthony asked.

"Is he in love or something?" Moseley asked.

Anthony shrugged his shoulders and Calvin nodded his head. "He forgot about the code. M.O.B, man. Money over bitches," Calvin answered.

"Once again, look who is talking," Anthony mumbled to Moseley.

I overheard Calvin's comment, stepped out the bathroom in a pair of boxers. "If y'all got something to say I'll respect y'all more as men if you said it to my face!" I hollered.

"And I'll respect you more if you was real nigga and had your boys' back!" Moseley said, challenging me.

"This is getting ugly," Anthony said.

"No, this is getting good," Calvin chuckled.

"Man, take your half-naked ass back in the bathroom!" Moseley snapped.

I replied, "Yeah, you should know a lil" something about that. I don't complain when you come out of your room naked!"

"Moseley? Naked?" Calvin asked. "Of course you don't complain. You should be used to seeing men naked."

"Calvin, I'm not even going to start with your dumb ass!" Khalid replied. "You don't know shit about what's going on. You stay talkin' that shit but never wanna get out there with me. Just stay bossing your woman around 'cuz that's what you do best." It was best that Calvin not be an instigator but mind his business.

"You so interested in my relationship, blood, you need to work on your own!"

"No nigga, your girl tells me what's going on in y'all relationship 'cuz she's so scared of your crazy ass!" I wanted Calvin to run up and swing on me, giving me a justification to fight. If anybody needed their ass beat it was Calvin, and I wanted to be the nigga to do it. Calvin didn't give into the harsh words.

"You tryna fight Calvin?" I decided to ask him.

"Nigga, I don't even respect you enough to fight you. You ain't even worth it. Matter of fact, you ain't worth shit. Get your life together and then we can talk. Try staying out of jail for a change. Take the loss and get right. I'm out, blood," Calvin said, leaving the house.

I was surprised that he was walking away from our confrontation. Sure, Dior didn't want Calvin fighting, but she was nowhere in sight.

As he left, Kiani was walking up the porch steps. I didn't want her to see me standing there in my boxers, feeling betrayed and disrespected by my boys. I told her I will be ready for her shortly and returned to the bathroom to continue getting ready.

"Well, do come in," Anthony said gentlemanlike. "Just have a seat. He'll be out soon."

Kiani sat down on the couch and waited patiently. Moseley and Anthony exchanged looks that said it all. They were silently giving each other the okay to ask Kiani some questions.

"Hey, Kiani?" Moseley said quietly. He scooted over to her on the couch and looked at Anthony. Anthony sat down on the couch across from them. Moseley continued, "How have you been?"

"I've been fine and you?"

"Good, just good. Um . . . I want to ask you something."

"Moseley, if this is about the 30s crip thing then I can't even discuss it with you. Khalid thinks it's best that I don't get involved," Kiani said, shooting down the conversation right away.

Moseley chuckled nervously and said, "Well, Khalid and I talked about all that the other day."

"What did he say?" Kiani asked.

"He said he would be cool with you talking to your cousin for me to find out who those crips were. But he said I couldn't ask you for any more information after that," Moseley lied.

"Well," said a hesitant Kiani. "All right. I can find that out. But this isn't going to come back to me, is it?"

"Hell nah. Khalid was just saying that to scare you out of it. 30s crips have so many niggas after their asses they won't know where to look. What's your cell phone number?" Moseley asked Kiani.

The naive Kiani gave him Moseley her number and he entered it into his cell phone. "I'll call you in a day or two to give you some time to talk to your cousin." He stood up, nodded at Anthony, and went into the kitchen. Moseley planned on what his next move would be and Anthony began to regret his role.

"All right, Kiani. Let's get the hell up out of here," I said coming into the living room moments later.

She stood up, said her good-byes to Anthony and Moseley and followed me out of the door.

Chapter Seventeen

Nyrique

A hot breeze knocked over the empty can of Pepsi on the porch step. Nyrique picked up the can and hauled it into the front yard. He let a wad of spit fly from his mouth and looked up into the cloudless sky, cursing the hot sun and the heat wave it bought to Southern California.

"Damn 'cuz! I finally got my girl to come stay with me for the weekend. You know I told her ass to stop talking to that slob Khalid. She did it and we haven't had a problem since then," Nyrique told Kevin, his crip friend who was released from jail three days ago.

"Khalid . . . Khalid. That name sounds familiar. Oh! That's, um —Hide! That nigga Hide!"

"Yup, him. And guess what? Some 20s bloods were at King Park not to long ago. We did a quick hit-'em-up and shot they asses! Killed one of them muthafuckas!" Nyrique laughed. "Why them niggas was at King Park anyway is a god damn mystery."

"Ah, for real? Who was you with?" Kevin asked trying, to catch up on all the hood drama he had missed for the last year of his life.

"Some of the homies . . . Derrick, TJ, and Mike. This crazy-ass blood had the mutha fuckin nerve to come up to us talkin' some loud shit! Mike shot his ass so quick he ain't even see that shit coming. Then his boy was a lil'' bitch. He didn't even come up with him, but wanted to fire from afar. I blasted on his ass too!" Nyrique bragged.

"Oh damn. Derrick's cousin Kiani come around anymore?" Kevin asked out of curiosity.

"That rich bitch?" Nyrique asked. "Hell nah, she keep her ass in them big-ass houses. She bet not bring her ass round this hood . . . or I'll have one of my bitches jack her ass for all she got."

"That ho was fine!" Kevin said, remembering her pleasant face when he saw her at Derrick's house. "Wonder what she been up to."

Nyrique shook his head "Nah, 'cuz! You remember Dior? Shay's best friend?"

Kevin gasped and said, "Sure do. I use to talk to her way back in the day, I mean way back. What she been up to?"

"According to Shay, she's with some blood name Calvin who be putting tabs on her. This dude flipped out on her because she wore some jewelry that her ex-boyfriend brought her," Nyrique laughed.

"And you flipped out on your girl for being friends with a blood," Kevin shot back. He sparked the end of his Black & Mild with his lighter. Once it was lit, he continued, "Fuck Calvin. Man, just one night and Dior will be having my baby."

"Funny you mentioned that. She's pregnant by o'boy too!"

Nyrique added. He knew it was better that Kevin know that detail now before trying to get at Dior.

Turned off by the fact that Dior was pregnant, Kevin shook his head disapprovingly and said, "Well then, fuck that. She's definitely off limits. But I'd still fuck her though."

Dior and Shay pulled up in front of the house in Dior's car. They had just come back from the doctor's office where she discovered she was three months pregnant and her baby was due May twentieth, right on time for summer vacation.

The doctor also told she needed to refrain from stressing herself out and invest her time in peaceful activities. When Dior asked if it was safe for her to have sex, the doctor laughed and said of course. Dior was going to tell Calvin, but it would be long into the pregnancy. Her plan was to hold out as long as she could . . . or until she started showing or Calvin asked.

"See you on Sunday" Shay said as she opened the car door to get out.

Nyrique saw the best friends waved each other good-bye before parting ways. Dior sped off in her car and Shay walked up the sidewalk toward the concrete porch where Nyrique and Kevin were sharing a beer. She grabbed Nyrique for a hug and in return he kissed her.

"Damn, do y'all wait?" Kevin said as they tongued each other down.

"In the presence of others," Shay told Nyrique as he palmed her ass. "Help me take my bags in, baby," Shay requested as she placed one of her bags in his hands.

"Hey Shay!" Kevin called out before the couple went into Nyrqiue's home. Once she replied, he asked, "You think you can put me down with Dior?"

"Again?" Shay said. "Kevin, she has a man."

"Yeah I know, and she's having his baby."

"How do you know?"

"Nyrique told me."

Shay, upset that Nyrique put private information into the ear of another, slammed the front door after trooping in.

She was hot on Nyrique's trail as he went into the bedroom and placed her bag in the corner. She threw her large purse on the edge of the bed.

"What the hell is your problem?" Nyrique asked, grabbing her arms. "You want it that bad? How sexually frustrated are you?"

"Nyrique, this isn't about sex. When I tell you something about me or Dior or anybody for that matter, it isn't meant for you to tell your friends," Shay answered angrily. The way she rolled her eyes and neck when she spoke let Nyrique know his girl had a major attitude.

"What the hell are you talking about?" Nyrique asked, laying down on his king-sized bed.

"How did Kevin find out about Dior's pregnancy? He just got out of jail and already knows the latest news. You have a big mouth," Shay hissed.

"You got a big mouth—literally."

Shay folded her arms across her chest and gave her boyfriend an evil glare. "You are so retarded, Nyrique. Don't broadcast information like that. Calvin doesn't even know. Why should Kevin?" she asked, shrugging her shoulders as if she was answering the question.

"So the fuck what?" Nyrique asked. "It's not like Kevin is going to tell Calvin. We don't like that slob."

"Yeah, yeah, whatever," Shay said nonchalantly.

Suddenly, a previous problem popped back into Nyrique's head. He asked, "Have you been speaking to Khalid?"

Shay shook her head and said, "No. For the last time . . . I told Khalid I was cool on him."

"Better had."

Shay sucked her teeth angrily. "You know what? I'm tired of you trying to boss me around. You need to change all of that, nigga. Damn!"

"Well, look who grew some balls in college. So which professor gave you the idea that it was smart to mouth off at your man?" Nyrique asked.

"No professor! I told myself it was okay, and please don't get it twisted! I been talking back, just not directly to you," Shay said, smirking.

"Well then to who?"

"Oh, I don't know. Khalid, maybe." Shay giggled, but was suddenly silenced when Nyrique slapped her dead across the face. She shrieked with pain, and clenched her fist with anger. Nyrique did not even apologize. He stood his ground, in his own defense and ready to do it again.

"Tha' fuck was that for?" Shay asked as she rubbed her stinging cheek with her hand.

"Your smart-ass mouth," Nyrique answered firmly. "It was gon'na happen sooner or later." There was no thought of apologizing in his mind. He felt Shay deserved what she got.

"Boy, you got me fucked up!" Shay said as she grabbed her bags and ran out the room.

Without saying another word, she ran down the porch stairs and never looked back. She walked to the bus stop and caught the bus to the next neighborhood over.

Shay was now knocking on the front door of the person she felt she needed most. She knew she had made a crucial mistake ending things with this person, being that he had cared about her and only wanted the best for them. She needed to apologize, and needed to hear him say he forgave her.

"Khalid! Khalid! Khalid."

I quickly ran to open the front door. It was Shay. She dropped her bags where she stood, fell into his arms, and bawled her eyes out.

I helped her into the house, leaving her bags on the front

porch. The only thing that was important to me was the state of Shay, and she was clearly in disarray.

"Shay, what's wrong?" Khalid asked, cradling her in my arms as they sat on the couch.

"Khalid, I am so sorry! I was stupid to walk out on our friendship! I am so sorry. I mean that, okay?" Shay asked, almost begging him for acceptance.

It was like a scene out of a movie and we were the main characters. The leading actress had realized her wrong, and came to her co-star to make it right and had no idea of what to do or say. Was this the climax?

"I forgive you, girl. I do. Now stop crying and tell me what happened," I said, sensing Shay was also crying for another reason other than their wobbly friendship.

"Nyrique hit me."

"What?"

"He hit me."

"When?"

"Like thirty minutes ago."

"Where?"

"At his house."

"Why?"

"He asked me if I was still talking to you. I said no, and then we got into it. He asked me why I was talking back to him. I answered with some smart-ass reply with your name in it. I was only joking and he slapped the shit out of me."

"Okay, slow down," I said, trying to process what I just heard. "You're talking hella fast, Shay. So basically, trying to be funny you said my name in a joke directed toward him and he slapped you for it."

Shay nodded her head, embarrassingly. "I'm so done with his ass. My mama said neva' let a man put his hands on you, and looka here . . . you ain't got to tell me twice! Fuck that nigga! I am so sorry I came at you like how I did with

Nyrique. I can't even believe I'd let Nyrique manipulate me like that," Shay apologized once more.

"So this means we're friends again?" I asked feeling relieved that Shay had her Nyrique wake-up call and got the message.

"We've always been friends. I've just been stupid," Shay responded. "Man, Khalid. You are—you are the sweetest person. I think—no, I know—I've been a bitch to you since you got out of jail. I regret all that, Khalid. And I've realized something else—"

"Shay," I interrupted her. "I think we should talk about this later."

"Why? I wanna talk about this now," she said.

Kiani came out from the bathroom, with a towel wrapped around her body. She had no idea Shay was in the living room with me until she heard the high-pitched voice.

"Khalid, I love you," Shay stated.

"What?" I asked. His eyes widened and jaw dropped at her revelation.

Shay clarified, "I love you as a best friend. I need you so much right now. You're so . . . man, I don't even know."

"Well, you better find out!" Kiani stepped into the conversation, and needed to know what the hell Shay was talking about.

I looked at Kiani and then at Shay. *Damn!* I thought. *I shoulda kept Kiani outside.* My heart was still soft for her, and seeing her in that fragile state at the front door confirmed that. I couldn't turn her away or leave her standing on the porch. I was in that weird, awkward situation again . . . the two women he cared for the most in his presence at the same time. I wanted to drop dead for this one moment . . . well, second moment.

"Excuse me?" Shay asked.

"Shay, we should really talk about this later," I insisted.

Shay shook her head and headed toward the door. She

was undoubtedly embarrassed that she came over to talk with me about something very personal and my girlfriend had heard a crucial part of our conversation. "Well, when you get the time, call me. You know my number," Shay said before leaving, looking at Kiani coldly. "Bye Khalid."

Kiani waited for Shay to be out of ear's reach and out the door before I heard, "Khalid, we need to talk."

Chapter Eighteen

Dior

Dior entered the house looking depressed and out of her element. She came in and went straight to the bathroom. She came out with red, teary eyes. There was no way I could ignore her, being that she appeared physically ill. I asked her what was wrong and she insisted it was bad allergies. But I've never known (or heard of) Dior to be allergic to anything except heartache and heartbreak. Being the concerned person I am, I wanted to know what it was that made things so depressing for her.

She was not the diva Dior on this day; she was depressed, deprived, and derailed. She went into Calvin's bedroom and when she saw he was not in there she came out with a worried look on her face. She looked up toward the ceiling while resting up against the wall of the hallway.

"Where's Calvin?" she asked, wiping away the tears in the corners of her eyes.

"He went to the store. Don't worry. You can talk to me if you have to. He won't be back for a little bit," I said humorously, hoping she would smile.

Dior frowned instead. She sniffled and wiped her slightly

ruddy eyes with the palms of her hands. "I'm not, Shay. My boyfriend will let me speak to you."

"Just not when he's around," I replied.

"No, just not about my relationship with him. That's all," Dior answered. She went to the couch and laid down on her back. She slowly ran her hand over her stomach. Back and forth. Back and forth. She was choking up with tears. "Khalid?"

"Yes?" I asked, sensing she wanted something.

"Can you get me some water please?" she asked.

"Sure. Are you feeling okay?" I asked. I stood up and walked into the kitchen. While retrieving a water bottle, I waited for her answer.

"Oh yes," she forced herself to say. "I'm fine."

I looked at her with a look of bewilderment. Even a blind person could see she wasn't fine. Dior was playing the role of something she was not—all right. I shook my head and gave her a concerned look that she could easily read.

"What, Khalid?" she asked, seeming annoyed. "Why are you looking at me like that?"

"I won't tell Calvin. I promise you. Now tell me what the hell is wrong with you," I demanded. "I promise that you'll feel better if you let it out."

Dior's eyes watered, and then came the tears, followed by the confession. "Khalid, I'm three months pregnant."

I wanted to say I knew it, but I didn't. In fact, I would've never guessed that. Finally, all their slipups caught up with them. "Well, congratulations," I said.

"No, not congratulations! To what? Fucking up my life? Khalid, I am in no position to have a baby and Calvin is in no position to take care of one. But I don't want to get an abortion."

"Why not?"

"I have morals."

"So women who get abortions don't have morals?"

"No, I'm not saying that," she answered. "Their morals are just different than mine." No arguing that. I handed her a box of tissues and waited for her next words. They were slow coming out and in a slight whisper. "He can't know. Please don't tell Calvin."

"You have my word. But why don't you want Calvin to know? This is his baby, isn't it?" I asked, hoping she wasn't fooling around on Calvin, something that would have shocked me to death if the answer was yes.

"Of course it's his! No fuckin' way it could be another's!" said a hostile Dior. "He'll force me to get an abortion."

"That's not true," I said. I wanted to take up for Calvin, but at the same time there was a strong likelihood of Calvin making Dior have the abortion.

"I know him, Khalid. If he doesn't want me to have this baby he will do what he has to do to make sure I don't!" she said.

I sighed angrily and responded, "So who is he to tell you what to do with your body? It's your body and the little life inside you is your responsibility."

"And it took two to make it so Calvin would feel obligated to make a decision."

"And only you could let it happen."

Dior was determined to keep it from Calvin. She made it official when she confirmed, "I'm waiting this pregnancy out as long as I can. If I start showing, I'll cover it up. But Calvin is not going to hear about it, at least not from me."

"So when will he be able to know?" I asked.

"When I'm five or six months, unless he finds out beforehand. So is my secret safe?"

I nodded my head and promised her I would not tell anyone about this. Dior, Shay, and I were the only ones who knew about the pregnancy. How convenient.

"I'll be asleep in his room when he comes in," Dior said as she stood up and walked into Calvin's bedroom.

Chapter Nineteen

Anthony

"*Seems like you're ready! Girl I know you're ready!*" sang a drunken Anthony. Other than R. Kelly's, his loud voice was heard over every other conversation.

The party he was throwing in Watts was going by just right. There were drinks, in which Anthony had too much of, weed, in which I wasn't smoking, and ladies, in which I didn't care to look at. My main lady was in my arms tonight. She looked sexy as hell in her little black mini-dress and BCBG heels. She swayed side to side to the music that Anthony continued to mess up the groove as he sang along, tangling up the words.

Moseley laughed, "Anthony, sit your ass down! Man, this dude is drunk as hell!"

His boys Nite, Slim, and Kush were posted up on the wall with him. They were part high and part drunk. Each wore red and black in different attire, but the same message came across. *Don't fuck with us 'cuz we're gangstas.*

The party lasted till about three in the morning, but Anthony's sobriety hadn't come back yet. A drunken Anthony hopped into the backseat of Kiani's car. He had finally said his fiftieth good-bye to Moseley and his boys.

"I hope he doesn't vomit in my car. I'm going to be pissed if he does," Kiani said.

"He'll be all right," I said, not believing that to be true.

Kiani pulled off slowly and vowed to drive slow the whole ride home. She didn't want Anthony to get motion sickness and vomit in the backseat of the car. She looked in the backseat periodically at the rarely drunk Anthony. Anthony babbled on, much about nothing. And then he went crazy.

"You know what, Khalid?" Anthony asked. "You are real lucky to have Kiani. She's sweet, polite, gorgeous, and rich and she hooked your ass up with a job. She's a keeper!"

"Don't I know it," I said, looking at Kiani as I got lost in thoughts of what I wanted to do to her when we reached her apartment that I had yet to move into. She blushed bashfully and told me to look away, and not at her.

"Nah, I'm for real, man!" Anthony slurred. "She even looked out for me and Mo. She told us about the cousin who was with 30s crips when they shot at Moseley!"

Kiani gasped and screamed, "Anthony!" She turned around and looked at him with fear in her eyes.

"Kiani, watch the damn road!" I hollered as I grabbed the steering wheel to keep the car from swerving into the next lane.

Anthony was cracking up hysterically in the back. As much as I wanted to slap the shit out of him, I was glad for this information. My thoughts went from sexing Kiani to strangling her. But I quickly pushed those crazy thoughts away. Kiani was stuck in her words, struck with guilt for betraying me.

"Khalid, baby, I am so sorry," she said calmly after she found the right words to say.

Though *sorry* was the word I wanted to hear, the calmness in her voice was not enough to calm my soul. Inside I was engulfed with rage, hurt, and pain. Kiani betrayed me on something so small. It wasn't worth it on her end. "You got involved in some unnecessary shit," I told her disapprovingly.

Kiani didn't utter a single sound or word. She was mute the whole ride home to my house. She parked, and waited for Anthony and me to get out of the car.

I opened the door and let the cool night air blow into the car. Exhausted from the thoughts running in my mind, I sighed heavily. Anthony managed to stumble out of the car and wobbled his way up the driveway and to the front door. I got out of the passenger side and looked over the hood of the car at Anthony, struggling to open the door with his key. I told myself to let him struggle; he deserved it for getting so drunk.

Kiani attempted to start the car back up, but the next word out of my mouth stopped her.

"Out," I stated.

She sighed significantly and took the keys out of the ignition. She got out of the car and followed me up the driveway and to the front door that Anthony still had not managed to get open. I took the keys from Anthony and opened the door myself. He ran straight into the bathroom and hurled vomit into the toilet. Kiani and I stayed in the living room. I looked at her, eyes saying every unimaginable thing I couldn't bring my lips to say. She spoke first.

"Khalid, he lied to me!" Kiani said.

"And you lied to me! What did I tell you? You said you wouldn't get involved in that!" I replied.

She shook her head and stated her case. "Khalid, please listen to me! Moseley and Anthony told me they talked to you and you said I could tell them! They seemed honest so I went ahead and told them who was there."

"Why the hell didn't you check with me first?" I asked.

Kiani shook her head and looked down at her feet as if the answer was on the floor. "I didn't think to ask you. I just believed them," she answered.

"You don't think much at all, do you?" I cruelly asked her, not giving a damn about how her feelings.

"That's a messed up thing to say to me," Kiani sadly replied.

"How do you allow yourself to be so easily deceived, Kiani? You mean to tell me that it never crossed your mind to ask me? That's crazy," I said, making sure she knew I was disappointed in her.

"I trusted them because they were your friends. So yeah, I guess that does make me a little naive. And I'm sorry," she said as she fought back tears. "I should have checked with you first."

"Yeah, you should have. So what did you tell them?" I asked, still trying to come to terms with how gullible Kiani was.

"I told them that it was these boys from 30s."

"Names?"

"TJ, Mike, and Nyrique."

"Nyrique?" I asked her, making sure I heard the right name.

"That's what I said."

"Where was your cousin?" I asked her.

"Oh, Derrick said he left before the gunshots were fired," Kiani informed. "I told them that too. I don't want my cousin getting fixed in that shit and he wasn't the one who pulled the trigger."

I shook my head, my eyes fixed to the floor. I couldn't even look at her because I was so upset with her actions. I wanted to change the hands of time and make things better for the future. But at this moment, I knew it was not happening. The battle had begun and I felt trapped in the center of the field.

Chapter Twenty

Calvin

Calvin clicked away furiously at the game controller as he played a virtual game of basketball against Evan.

"Man, you getting' served right now, blood!" Calvin bragged.

"You just got your goodluck charm here! That's all," Evan said, referring to Dior, who was reading a pregnancy magazine. Calvin turned around to look at her, sitting in between his arched forward body and this couch. She sat comfortably as her eyes gazed through the pages of a magazine she could relate to.

"What are you reading?" Calvin asked as he snatched the magazine out of her hands.

"Hey! Give that back!" Dior shouted as she tried to retain the magazine.

"*Pregnancy* magazine? What the fuck? What's wrong with you?" Calvin asked. "Reading a pregnancy magazine?"

"Nothing, Calvin. I'm reading it for class," Dior said with watery eyes.

"You're not pregnant, are you? And why are you about to cry? What's wrong with you?" he asked with an attitude.

"Could you please stop asking me that?!" Dior screamed. She got up and ran to the bathroom. She slung her body over the tub rail and released vomit into the bathtub.

Calvin and Evan looked at each other, both confused at Dior's outburst and dramatic exit.

Calvin shook his head and said, "Her ass has been so damn emotional lately! Every little thing makes her want to cry. I'm about to look in her purse to see if she's on drugs or something!" Though Evan laughed like it was a joke, Calvin was dead serious. He grabbed the purse and skimmed through it. "She is on drugs!" He lifted up the bottle of pills and read the label. "Prenatal vitamins."

"Those are the pills they gave my sister . . . when she was pregnant," Evan informed.

Angrily, Calvin got up and stormed to the bathroom and found Dior throwing up. "Dior? You're pregnant?" he asked, upset that she was pregnant and that she didn't tell him sooner.

Dior wiped the remains of puke from her mouth with a paper towel. She looked up at Calvin hovering over her. "I'm sorry I didn't tell you!"

"And why the fuck not?"

" 'cuz you would have made me get an abortion," Dior answered honestly.

"Damn right! We're not ready for a damn baby!" Calvin yelled.

"Please stop yelling at me. I already have a headache," wailed Dior. She rose to her feet and grabbed his hands. "Baby, I just couldn't tell you yet."

"So you was gon'' hide this from me? You crazy, girl! Crazy in your head to think I wouldn't have found out!"

"Well, I must've been doing good 'cuz I got away with it this long," Dior snapped.

Calvin grabbed her by the collar of her shirt and stood her up. Dior slapped his face with her wet hands. Now that she was pregnant, there were some things that Calvin was not going to get away with and that included roughing her up. The look on his face showed he was shocked by this.

"Don't ever put your hands on a pregnant woman . . . especially when the baby is yours!" Dior yelled, pointing her index finger at him. "You're crazy! Must be out of your fuckin' mind to think I'ma put up with this shit now that I'm pregnant! Hell nah." She pushed Calvin out of her way and left the bathroom.

Calvin, now confused and distraught, sat on the edge of the bathtub as he held his head down and hunched his shoulders, showing signs of a lingering insecurity. Thoughts of how his life would change forever raced through his mind like a movie being fast-forwarded. The more he thought about it, the more he realized he was at a serious turning point in his life. What was he going to do now that he was soon to be a father?

Undoubtedly, life was out of order. It was unplanned. In Calvin's mind, he knew what the easy solution was. Abortion. But at this point, Dior was far down the line and she would fight for what she wanted, which was to keep their baby.

Evan knocked hesitantly on the bathroom door.

"Yeah," Calvin mumbled.

Evan asked, "Is everything okay? Dior just stormed out of the house like she was crazy. What's going on, man?"

"What the fuck do you think is going on? She is pregnant! And she ain't getting an abortion. My life is over," Calvin told his cousin.

Evan whistled. "Daaa-yum! What the fuck are you going to do with a baby?"

Calvin shrugged and answered, "I don't know. My job alone can't support me, her and a kid. And she's in school and can't support the baby alone. I refuse to leave her. I ain't that kind of guy, you know."

Evan nodded and asked, "I feel you, but what are you going to do?"

Calvin looked at Evan with anguish in his eyes. "What am I supposed to do? I can't tell her not to have the baby. She's going to have it regardless of what I feel. I just wish it was under different circumstances."

"Well, you still tryna see me on the game, man?" Evan asked, wanting to get back to the game of NBA Live he had paused on the PS3.

"Nah, let me go try to fix things with my lady," Calvin said as he rose to his feet. He left the bathroom and grabbed his jacket. "I'll call you later." He rushed out the door and to his car.

Calvin started the car and drove down the street toward Western Avenue, where Dior was waiting at the bus stop. Her face was red with tears and sadness was written all over her. Calvin hated seeing her like that, and knowing she was pregnant with his child only worsened the situation. What kind of man would he be to leave his lady alone? He'd be a stereotype. Another man in the group of deadbeat baby fathers.

I'm not about to abandon my girl and my child, Calvin thought. He had common sense, and right now it was telling him to be there for his girlfriend. He rolled down his window to speak to her. "Dior, what kind of man would I be to not want this for us? So what it came sooner than we wanted. I love you, and I already love that baby."

Dior wiped her eyes as her boyfriend said words that made her melt. Calvin asked her to get in the car. She willingly got in the passenger seat, grateful that she did not have to catch the bus. Calvin placed his hand over Dior's belly. She leaned her head back and grinned.

"It's going to be a beautiful thing, baby" Dior said.

And in his heart, Calvin totally agreed.

Chapter Twenty-one

Kiani

The warehouse morning shift came to a close. Employees rushed to finish the last of their work, whether it was moving boxes, parking the forklift, or packaging up a shipment. Today wasn't a good day for me. All I had been thinking about the past couple of days was where I stood with Kiani. She consistently called, but I would decline to answer. I forgave her for her mistake of telling Moseley who it was who shot him, but I needed time to myself to get over it.

It was three o'clock and I clocked out on time. Me and a coworker that I planned to get a ride with stepped out of the warehouse building and into the hot sun. The unbearable weather still hadn't let up, and we were starting to feel it. There had already been a series of wildfires in the valley, and the city was racking up millions of dollars in damages. On top of that, the California Water Resources was predicting a critical water shortage and wanted the people's help in taking action. But if they thought that crisis was going to force people to use less water in this heat, they were wrong.

My coworker handed me a water bottle. I proceeded to follow him to his car, but I was stopped by the sight of Mr. Wesley's car, with Kiani in the driver's seat. She honked the horn as if she didn't see me coming over.

"Hey, Khalid, you coming with me?" my coworker asked.

I shook my head. "Guess not!" I got into the passenger seat and heavily sighed out a long day's work.

"How was work?" Kiani asked. Her voice was pleasant. I knew it was an attempt to get on my good side . . . not that one existed at this point in my life. Kiani used to be the center of my serenity—but not anymore. Her betrayal cut deep. As little as it seemed, one mess-up could mess it *all* up. She wasn't only to blame. Moseley played a major role in this by milking the information out of her.

"How long have you been waiting out here?" I asked her instead of answering her question.

"Since two o'clock," she answered.

I looked at her with both eyebrows raised. "You mean to tell me you've been waiting out here since two o'clock? A whole hour in this car?"

Kiani nodded bashfully like she had done something wrong. "I just needed to talk to you. You haven't called me since the night of Anthony's party. I know your feelings are hurt, but so are mine, Khalid," she said with her eyes fixed on the steering wheel.

"Kiani," I began. "Do you love me?"

She looked up slowly and answered, "Yes, I do. I am so sorry that I told Moseley that information. If I would've known, then I—"

An endearing kiss hushed her up. I cupped her face in my hands and noticed she was warm from blushing. I tried not to blush myself as our tongues caressed in a way that I missed over the past three days.

"I love you too," I said. I meant it—from the *L* to the *E*.

"Can we go home?" Kiani asked. "And make love?" A seductive grin appeared on her round face.

My dick instantly firmed up. I smiled, and that was her answer. We were at her house in her bed in no time.

I climbed on top and proceeded inside of her. She gasped and whispered intop my ear how good it felt.

"Baby," she moaned. "I want you to make me cum in ways I never imagined."

A kiss sealed the deal and we made love. It was passionate, it was real, and it was love. This was a new experience for both me and her. This union had reached a whole new level. After we both climaxed in harmony, we lay there staring into each other's eyes. I memorized every facial expression, movement, and any detail in-between about her. She was truly beautiful. We had progressed so much that I often forgot how we met. I forget how she ended my hunt for females because she was the treasure. I was in love . . . and it felt good.

"Khalid, love," Kiani said softly.

"Hmm?"

"What's the deal with Shay?"

Why would she ruin this moment? I thought to myself. I answered, "Shay is a very good friend of mine. I used to like her back in the day, but she didn't want to be with me because I was gangbanging. So I got out of jail, tryna do good, wanted to hook up with her but she had a boyfriend."

"So when she told you she loved you, what was that about?" Kiani asked.

"She had broken up with him. But I don't think you should worry yourself with that. I love you and only you. You hear me?"

"I don't want to feel threatened," Kiani said. "I'm scared that I might lose you."

I pulled her hair from out of her face. "There's no need

to be scared. I will do everything that I can to make sure you feel secure with me." But even with the firmness in my voice, I didn't trust that answer.

Certainly I did feel Shay as a threat, and there was always the possibility that she could grab hold of the vulnerable part of me. No matter how far apart we became, there was always a place for Shay in my heart. I realized that I was torn between two women for the first time. They had stripped down the wall I had built up to guard my inner man, and I had definitely built a wall around my emotions. They saw right past the thugged-out nigga who had been to jail three times. Each of them saw the real me differently, and now I was battling to keep one of them in and the other out.

Chapter Twenty-two

Moseley

Nite, Slim, and Kush waited impatiently outside of the St. Andrews apartment complex. They thought it would take Moseley less than a minute to go into the home of Casey, the OG who had the gun hookup, grab three semi-automatics and return to the Caprice they waited in.

"Moseley needs to hurry up! I'm ready to let these niggas have it. Any nigga on the block is gettin' it!" Slim said. He found pleasure in drive-bys and honor in protecting his gang's reputation.

"It's either go hard or go home," Kush replied.

Nite agreed and added, "Hell yeah, blood. They fucked with the wrong group of niggas when they killed my cousin Jordan." He had recently got *R.I.P Jordan Knightly* on his forearm, and was down for revenge when Moseley came to him regarding the death of his cousin.

Moseley exited the apartment with a black gym bag stuffed with three semiautomatics and gun clips. He hopped into the passenger seat. "A tech-nine, and two AK-forty-sevens," Moseley said, naming the guns he was given inside Casey's apartment.

"Bullshit, bullshit, and mo' bullshit. I knew Casey was gon' give us something average. We gotta make a quick stop," Kush said, disapproving of the guns Moseley announced.

"Where we headed?" Moseley asked him. "Shit, I'm ready to ride out and you wanna make stops?"

Kush sparked a cigarette and answered his anxious friend, "My Uncle Boogie from Van Ness Gangsters house. That mu'fucka say he got a gun he want me to try out."

"Damn, Boogie, you said?" Moseley asked, the name sounding very familiar to him.

Kush inhaled the cigarette smoke and blew it out the window of the Caprice. He started up the car and backed out of the parking space. "How do you know him?" he asked.

"That's that nigga Hide's big homie," Moseley informed. "You know Hide, use to be from Van Ness? He introduced me to him back in the day. I almost wanted to get put on Van Ness back in the day." Moseley could picture Boogie's face. Chipmunk cheeks, beady eyes with a tattooed tear on the left, side and the blackest lips he had ever seen.

"That's Hide's big homie? I'm sure Boogie will be glad to hear he's going good," Nite chimed in.

"Don't you think he already knows that? Hide probably talks to him everyday," Slim said. "Don't he, Mo?"

Moseley shrugged his shoulders in reply, although he knew the answer.

When I said I was done with gangbanging, I meant it. I hadn't heard from or seen my old gangbanging buddies Pablo, Rock, and Aaron since the party in Inglewood. I also never visited my big homie Boogie.

Moseley hoped Boogie wouldn't remember his face from the first time they met and ask him about me. That was a position he didn't want to be put in.

"Hell nah, that nigga probably don't talk to him. You

know Hide—excuse me, Khalid—went all soft on niggas and quit that gangbanging shit. He ain't gangsta no mo'," laughed Nite. He rolled down his window as Kush drove out of the complex gate and onto Adams Boulevard.

"Oh yeah, that's funny?" asked Kush. "And when you plan on gettin' out the lifestyle?"

Nite sucked his teeth and answered the question. "C'mon now, you know the shit don't stop til the casket drop."

Moseley shook his head at his friend. "Shit, I don't blame that nigga, though. He been through a lot. I ain't surprised he really changed this time," he said, taking up for his friend.

"Whatchu tryna say? You want out too?" Nite asked angrily.

"I didn't say that, nigga. I can just see where Khalid is coming from," Moseley answered defensively.

Nite nodded his head in approval. "Well good, 'cuz we got work to put in tonight, blood."

Moseley remained quiet the rest of the trip to Boogie's house. He knew the location. It was the same area where me and my boys had committed that robbery, and sent me to jail for three years.

Kush parked the car on the street and lit a second cigarette before getting out of the car. Once he noticed no one had got out the car as he did, he requested that Moseley come with him.

"C'mon, Mo. Roll wit' me," he said with the cigarette still in his mouth.

Moseley sighed, making it apparent that he did not want to go inside. He followed Kush up to the front door of his uncle's home. Kush knocked twice, and they were greeted by the end of a sawed-off shotgun.

"Nigga, what the fuck you want?" Boogie asked, aiming the shotgun at his nephew's head. Their was a brief pause, in which Moseley almost pissed in his pants.

Boogie let out a laugh and set the shotgun up against the wall. "Hey nephew, what's good with you?"

"Shit, Boogie! Don't be pointing no damn gun at me, blood!" Kush laughed, shaking his uncle's strong hand.

Boogie looked at Moseley, still wearing the horrified look on his face. "And look at this nigga," he laughed. "Scared than a muthafucka. C'mon in here, man. It's all good. My daughter went out on a date and I had to scare the punk muthafucka straight with this." Boogie closed the front door and picked up the shotgun.

"I know you ain't giving me that to use tonight," Kush said, disapproving of what he thought was his uncle's surprise.

Boogie looked at him as if he was joking. He began, "Now you know your uncle better than, that lil' nigga. Hell nah, this right here is my baby. Don't nobody use this but me. What I got to show you is in the basement. C'mon and follow me."

Kush and Moseley followed Boogie into the basement of the house. Boogie's home was an older home, and one of the few homes in Los Angeles that had a basement. In the red-light basement there were a variety of guns mounted on the wall. Underneath them were cases, also full of different types of guns. Moseley suspected that Boogie sold these guns to other gangbangers.

"Damn," Moseley accidently let escape from his mouth.

Boogie looked back at Moseley, who was in awe. "Nice collection, ain't it. Can't tell you where I get my hookup from but anytime you need a weapon, I gotchu, blood. You a friend of Kush, you a friend of mine."

Kush, admiring the guns on the wall, added, "Yeah, Uncle. Y'all met way back in the day. He's friend with your lil' homie Hide."

Damn, Kush. Why you got to go running your mouth?

Moseley thought as he anticipated what Boogie was going to say next.

"Get outta here! Hide? Went to jail almost four years ago for robbing that corner store?" Boogie asked.

"Yeah, that's him," Kush answered on Moseley's behalf.

"You heard from him lately?" Boogie asked Moseley.

"Um—" Moseley was cut off by Kush's answer.

"Hide moved in with Mo when he got out," Kush said.

"For real?" Boogie said, surprised at this news. "Hide was a friend, man. I was real hurt when he got locked up. I wanted to go visit him but none of the otha lil' youngstas had his info. Said he wasn't calling or nothing."

"Nah, Hide told me he was calling and they weren't taking his calls," Moseley said, feeling now it was appropriate to converse with Boogie.

"That's strange. Well, why he ain't never came over here to say wassup? I'm his big homie. I asked about him. Pablo, Rock, and Aaron said they saw him at a party and he disrespected the hood. I don't know what the fuck is going on with him," Boogie said with concern. "Here, take my card and tell him to give me a call. I'd really like to talk to him. See how he doin' and all."

Moseley took the business card Boogie handed him. He glanced at it and saw that Boogie was a handyman by day. That would account for all the nice work done in the basement. "Yeah, no doubt. I'll let him know," Moseley replied.

"Now, back to business . . . where is this gun at Boogie?" Kush asked as he rubbed his hands together anxiously.

Boogie grabbed a large suitcase from underneath a table. He set the suitcase on top of the table and decoded the number lock that kept the suitcase from being opened by anyone else. Kush's eyes lit up when Boogie held up the firearm.

"What the fuck is that?" asked an excited Kush.

"KP forty-four Pistol. This shit ain't no joke either,

youngsta. This that *Call of Duty: World At War* shit!" Boogie said as he pointed the gun at the wall.

"Sure is the gun from that game," Moseley said with a smile. He played that game faithfully, and would pretend he was in war when he went through with his revenge tonight.

"All right, give it here," Kush said, trying to take the weapon from his uncle.

"You gon" do a drive, by with no bullets, youngsta?" Boogie asked him.

Kush rolled his eyes angrily and said, "Well, show me how to load it, and hurry up!"

"Easy there," Boogie said as he retrieved the bullets from the drawer of the table. He loaded the gun for his nephew and handed it over.

"Damn, I'm finna do some damage with this," Kush said. He was grateful he had one of the better guns out of his boys. "I might come out with the win tonight."

"Y'all lil' niggas get out of here . . . and be safe aight. Watch out for the pigs. They everywhere nowadays, and they jut waiting to lock y'all black asses up," Boogie said.

The men headed up the stairs and back into the living room. Kush thanked his uncle once more before putting the gun in a duffel bag.

Moseley shook hands with Boogie and said, "Good lookin' out, man. I'll tell Hide to hit you up."

"Yeah, make sure you do that," Boogie said. He watched the boys head down the walkway and get into the Caprice.

"All right boys, let's go to work," Kush said, gently handing Nite, in the passenger seat, the duffel bag.

Kush and Slim traded places, Kush getting in the backseat and Slim getting behind the wheel. Kush wanted to be one of the men to shoot, and the one to drive off. With this gun, he planned to do damage when he opened fire. Slim promised that wouldn't drive the way he normally would, very fast and with a blunt in his mouth. He didn't need to attract attention to the already stereotyped car they were in. He knew at this time of night the police were only looking out for black males. The ones driving in wide-body cars with rims, hydraulics, and other tricked out car gear would be the first to be targeted.

Moseley noticed the time—1:59 AM. It was a Saturday so he knew the 30s crips were out . . . hopefully at King Park. One street passed, and another and another. They were nearing 30s hood. Moseley internally counted the blocks. Fifty-fourth . . . Forty-second . . . Western Avenue . . . Thirty-sixth . . . Thirty-ninth. Right turn. King Park.

"There they go. They're walking down the street," Kush said as he pointed out the four boys parading Thirty-ninth Street.

"How do you know it's them, blood?" Moseley asked. His voice was shaky and he was sweating bullets. His palms were sweaty, so sweaty the gun could have slipped out of his hands if he didn't have a strong enough grip.

"What do you mean, how do I know? Who gives a fuck! They're crips, so fuck em! Let's do this shit!" Kush said, bringing the car to an even slower creep.

"Nah, that's them, all right. I know Nyrique black ass from anywhere. Let's go blood, now!" Nite said as he rolled down the window.

Moseley followed suit and did the same. As Slim turned the car headlight's off, Kush rolled down the right-side back window and prepared himself to aim and shoot. Moseley sat up in the left-side window where he could shoot over the hood of the car.

Nite, ready to fire in the passenger seat, sounded off the attack. "Let's go, blood!" he shouted.

A line of gunshots followed. Derrick, TJ, Mike, and Nyrique ran for cover and for their lives. Windows of nearby cars were shattered by the fired shots and alarms sounded off simultaneously. There was an disturbance of peace in the neighborhood. Slim pressed on the gas and wheeled off Thirty-ninth Street.

All the nervousness Moseley had felt prior to the drive-by had disappeared. He felt more gangsta than ever. He had never knew what it felt like to have an adrenaline rush, but he did now thanks to the drive-by. His heart pumped with excitement, feeling like going another round. He felt victorious.

"You think we got them niggas?" Moseley asked, looking out the back window.

"Hell yeah, we got them niggas!" Kush said. "I seen one of 'em fall."

"We better had got them niggas! That's on my cousin Jordan. I'ma make sure them bitches are dead!" Nite promised.

The next sound they heard was a helicopter and police sirens that seemed a few blocks away.

"C'mon, y'all. Let's get our asses home," Moseley suggested.

Chapter Twenty-three

Kevin

Shay received the call at the dorm in the early morning. Nyrique had been shot five times, twice in the leg, three times in the arm. It was by the grace of God he lived. TJ and Mike, miraculously, were able to dodge every bullet that came their way. Derrick, however, wasn't so fortunate. He was hit by seven bullets and the one to his heart ended his life.

Shay almost passed out when Kevin told her the news. "Kevin, don't lie to me!" she exclaimed. "This is a joke, right?"

"Shay, I swear I am not lying. Nyrique is at Kaiser right now. You just better be grateful he's not dead!" Kevin told her. He insisted he was telling the truth and Shay finally believed him.

Shay tossed the phone down and went to the bathroom. Dior, who was listening the whole time, got out of her bed and grabbed the phone.

"Who is this and what did you say to my friend?" asked a more than concerned Dior.

"Who is this?" Kevin asked, but he already knew it was Dior.

"Dior, her best friend," she replied combatively.

Kevin chuckled with amusement and Dior demanded to know what was so funny. "Nothing, really. Is this what our first conversation is going to be like?" he asked. A mushy grin appeared on his face.

"Who is this? Kevin?" Dior asked. She received no reply. Definitely Kevin. "Hey, how are you, Kevin?" She found the nerve to smile mischievously.

"I'm fine. How about you?" he asked, trying not to let the excitement he was feeling be heard in his voice.

"I'm okay, I guess," Dior said with uncertainty. " But I would like to know what's going on."

"Nyrique was shot, probably by some bloods from 20s or some Mexicans. But he's gon'na make it," Kevin answered. "How is it coming with the baby?"

"Kevin, how do you know about that?"

"Is me finding out about your baby a bad thing?" he asked so smoothly it gave Dior the chills.

Now she was flustering over her words. "No, it's not that. It's not that it's a bad thing. I just rather—"

"You just rather tell me yourself," Kevin cleared.

Dior agreed and said, "Yes, Kevin, that would've been better. I am about four and a half months pregnant. I go to the doctor at the end of this week to see what I am having."

"It's Calvin's?" Kevin asked.

"Only Calvin's," Dior replied.

Kevin groaned. Now that they were talking, Kevin's deeply buried history with Dior had resurfaced. Kevin could only wish she was pregnant with his child. "So being that you have a baby on the way, you definitely don't have any time to go out with an old friend."

"No, Kevin. I can't do that," Dior said, puzzled by his question. "How can you come at me like that so easily?"

Kevin was puzzled as well. Dior could tell by the way he answered the question. "What the fuck do you mean? Damn, I wasn't asking to be with you!"

"Fuck you, Kevin! Some things never change. Like how you talk to me! That's one of the hundred and eighty-six reasons why we aren't together!" Dior replied inimically. Her face flushed with redness.

"For real, Dior? So why do you let Calvin treat you like a dog? From what I heard he has you on a tight leash," Kevin snapped back, trying to anger his ex-girlfriend.

His comment had an adverse effect. Dior's pregnant-influenced attitude showed its capriciousness as it went from angry to calm. "Kevin, let's not argue. There's been enough drama for both of us to bear. Lord knows I don't need all this stress on my baby."

"You got that right. I don't know what I'd do if my boy Nyrique didn't make it," Kevin agreed. "Do you think the baby will bring you guys closer?"

"I'm not sure. I've known some people who have been torn apart because of a baby.

It can either go one or two ways. We'll just have to find out now, won't we?" Dior asked.

"Well, if the baby tears you all apart then you can get closer to me," Kevin joked. But he knew that Dior didn't find it at all amusing.

The odd moment of silence followed. Kevin broke it up. "Well, take my number down."

"Why, Kevin?" Dior asked rejecting, his request, even though she had already taken her cell phone off the charger.

"So we can talk and get reacquainted with each other. Maybe one day we can hang out. Let's go baby shopping or something," Kevin suggested.

"All right," Dior said reluctantly. She took down Kevin's number and stored it in her phone. "But just to go baby shopping," she joked.

"You got it," Kevin replied cheerfully.

"Well, now I am going to go check on my best friend. I guess I'll talk to you later."

Kevin and Dior hung up the phone. Kevin walked back into the house and climbed back in the bed with last night's treat. She didn't even notice he had got out of bed. He laid down on his back with his hands fixed behind his head and looked up at the ceiling.

He could remember the days of his innocence . . . about six years back. He was only fourteen. Although familiar with gangbanging, he never got acquainted. Kevin was the nerd on the block. The kid who was always at the basketball court, but was never passed the ball. The kid who was in class, while his friends were ditching. Kevin grew accustomed to his image and how he was treated.

As freshman year approached, Kevin wanted to change his Goody Two shoes behavior to bad-boy status. He was always pressured into joining the clique 2-Nasty crip because it would toughen up his image. Nobody wants to stay the good boy forever.

A few days before making it official to get jumped into the clique, Kevin met Dior. Dior was the first person— other than his pious grandmother— to make Kevin feel special just the way he was. She liked his good behavior and kind nature. For the first time, Kevin felt complete.

By end of sophomore year, Dior and Kevin had ended a young relationship over Kevin selling drugs for his thug Uncle Maury. That's when all hell broke loose. Kevin turned into a whole new person. He joined 30s crip gang and went crazy from selling drugs to using them. He went to jail for possession of illegal weapons and drugs when he was pulled over by the cops for driving with his headlights off at night. He was sentenced to two years in prison.

Those two years in prison are what kept Kevin sane. He got his life back together and was ready to start new. The start would be so much better if he had Dior on his side. Hopefully, he could correct some of the wrongs of the past—and that meant correcting his relationship with Dior.

Chapter Twenty-four

Nyrique

It seemed as if the earth has recognized the death of Derrick. It was a rare, gloomy Saturday morning in Los Angeles. Gray clouds with no silver lining slathered the sky to pour out rain. Kiani, although dressed in black, still appeared radiant. It was something natural, obviously. I looked in the corner of her eye and there was a tear. *Angels do cry*, I thought to myself. I held her hand and hoped that was enough to comfort her for the next few minutes. I was used to the funeral process. Death was a numbing phenomenon. I didn't feel happy or sad about it. It is what it is. Unlike me, Kiani has never dealt with death up close. It was my duty to assist her.

She looked at me with her lips tightly closed. They converted into a forced smile. I couldn't help but smile back and kiss her on the forehead. We got into her car. I offered to drive and headed toward the church. Then she began to question me about death.

"You've been to a funeral, right?" she asked.

"A lot of 'em," I answer while concentrating on the road.

"How many?"

"A lot. Too many to remember."

"Are you scared of death, Khalid?"

"Nope."

She gasped and asked, "Why not?"

"I've looked death in the face, Kiani. When it's my time, it's my time. Sometimes I feel like I'm dying, life is so damn hard. But I'm still here . . . so til then, I'll live life."

"That's a horrible thing to say."

"Why?"

"Everyone is afraid to die. They just don't admit it."

"No, not everyone is afraid to die. It's just nobody wants to."

"And you're not scared of dying?" Kiani asked in disbelief.

"No, not at all," I answered wholeheartedly. "Those who ain't afraid to die, don't."

"You better find God or Allah or Buddha or something because death is real. Once you're gon', that's it!" Kiani replied.

I shrugged my shoulders. She sucked her teeth and shook her head in astonishment.

Once we arrived at the church, Kiani forced herself to seem content and I forced myself to be calm. In reality, my heart was pounding with anger as the fact that my friend had something to do with this death dawned on me. Derrick rolled around with 30s crips. And while he might not have been a gang member, he sure was guilty by association. Now dead. After Kiani leaked that tip to Moseley, he took immediate action. When I got home, Moseley and I had some serious talking to do.

Kiani and I walked up to the open casket that should only remain open until the service started. She kept her head low as we took a trip down the middle aisle. I could see Derrick from here. Unrecognizable. Face swollen, eyes shut, mouth poked. Death has so many faces.

"Oh my God!" Kiani screamed when she saw Derrick lying in the casket. "Oh God! Oh God, why?"

All eyes were on us as I tried to hold Kiani in place. Kiani fought to grab ahold of Derrick in the casket. It took every ounce of strength in me to keep her in my grasp. I was getting weaker as she got angrier. All the strength and anger she now had came from within. I kept telling myself, *Khalid, let her go, let her go.* I did just that. She covered the top half of the casket with her arms. She laid there and cried. Just like the rest of the congregation, I just gazed at her with sorrow. Nothing I could do or say would bring Derrick back. Therefore, I let her go through her personal grieving process. The pallbearers gently grabbed her and removed her off of her dead cousin's body.

Kiani turned around and looked at the congregation like they were the murderers. Her face lacked expression and was a ruddy color. She buried her face into her hands and ran out the sanctuary. I jogged after her.

"Kiani! Baby? You'll be okay, Kiani. I promise," I told her as I rocked her in my arms.

"I know, I know," she sniffled. "I'm just so lost. I'm hurt! I'm confused! I'm scared, Khalid. I had something to do with this, didn't I?" Her voice came down to a slight whisper.

"Nah, baby. This isn't your fault," I answered.

Kiani wiped her eyes with the sleeve of her blouse. "Don't lie in church," she told me. "I already know it's partly my fault. Had I not given Mo that info my cousin would still be alive. And you warned me . . . that's the part that really hurts me. Had I listened to you none of this would have happened."

"Come here," I said, extending my hand out. We held

hands as I tried my best to console her. "Truthfully speaking, Kiani, Moseley was going to find out who it was that shot him whether or not you told him. I don't know who would have told him but he just found out sooner from you."

"It is my fault." Kiani had her mind made up that she was the reason her cousin was in a casket.

I had felt how she was feeling before, holding me responsible for the actions of others. Anthony gave me the best piece of advice, and I felt it was appropriate to pass that on to Kiani.

"Kiani, don't blame yourself for other people's actions. Moseley and them made their own decision, and it was the wrong one. How were you to know, Derrick was going to be with them? It was accidental that Derrick got shot, all right? And that's life, we just got to move on from here," I said.

I kissed her forehead and held her even closer to my chest. The moment I looked up I saw Nyrique hobbling toward us in crutches. His eyes were red, which either meant he had shed some tears of his own or was high off of a blunt. I loosened my grip on Kiani and cleared my throat. You would've thought she had read my mind the way she turned around.

"My condolences," Nyrique said as he grabbed Kiani's hand and kissed it. "Derrick was a really good person."

"Thank you," Kiani said as she reached for him in a hug.

A small part of me grew jealous—something absolutely new. Never have I allowed myself to get envious of another guy touching my girl. But this came natural. I couldn't help it. Nyrique snuck a look at me as he and Kiani separated. He stuck his hand out. I shook it. When releasing my hand he threw up his hood. What he didn't know was that I couldn't care less where he was from.

"How you holdin' up, Kiani?" Nyrique asked. She nodded. "If you need anything—anything at all—you be sure to call me."

Kiani took a step back into me. She searched for my hand. Once she found it, she raised it waist-high so Nyrique saw it. That was all that needed to be done to show that she and I were together, and I was all she needed.

Nyrique licked his lips, seeming more embarrassed than sincere. "Can I promise you something?" Nyrqiue asked her. "I swear on my life and on Derrick's grave—may he rest in peace. I will find whover killed your cousin. All right?" Nyrique's eyes instantly shifted toward me. He continued, "And whoever did it will pay . . . okay?"

Kiani didn't answer verbally, but she stared at Nyrique which said she wanted the job done. It was not the time or place for me to say anything, but I saw the death cycle repeating all over again.

Chapter Twenty-five

Moseley

As we left the funeral, the sun found its away among the gray clouds and graced us with its warmth. Just when we were grateful for the rain, the sun made a special appearance, letting us know he was still in the business of heating up California.

Kiani dropped me off back at the house, but couldn't stay because she had to work. I gave her a kiss on the cheek before exiting the car. Her spirit seemed lifted; the complete opposite of what it was this morning before the funeral. She honked her horn and waved good-bye to me before she drove off. Things started to move slowly now as I turned and entered the house. The walk down the hallway seemed longer than usual. I made it to Moseley's filthy room where I found him laying on his bed, naked.

"Damn it, man!" I said, quickly shielding my eyes. "Put some clothes on. I need to talk to you."

"Okay, talk," he said. His room appeared as if a tornado swept through it. There were clothes everywhere, including a pair of jeans slung over the television. I could barely see the carpet on the floor thanks to the piles of dirty laundry.

"Put on some shorts or something!" I demanded.

With an irritated sigh, Moseley located the nearest pair of shorts and slid into them. He responded, "There, Khalid. I'm covered up. Now what's going on?"

After removing a T-shirt from the seat, I sat down in his desk chair and began, "I respect you, Moseley. I got nothing but love for you. That's why I'm going to come at you straight-up, man-to-man." Pause. "Did you have anything to do with Derrick's murder?"

"Man, don't come at me with that bullshit!" Moseley yelled.

"Bullshit?" I asked in disbelief. "Moseley, somebody was murdered over this so-called bullshit! I'm being straight-up and I want you to tell me."

"Straight-up? Fuck that! Khalid, you're meddling. The only reason you actually give a fuck is 'cuz of that bitch Kiani. If she wasn't in the picture this would just be another case of gangbanging shit. Get the fuck outta here," Moseley argued.

"Kiani? You think this is all about Kiani? Nigga, this is about your life. Don't act like Derrick's peoples are just sitting quiet about this. Just like y'all didn't sit on Jordan's death, they not gon' sit on Derrick's death. You next in line if you keep fucking with this gangbanging shit."

Moseley laughed, throwing me off guard. "Look who's talking! Mr. Went to Jail Three Times and Came Out a Fuckin' Saint. Nigga, you ain't no saint. Once a thug, always a thug. Why you runnin' away from your past knowing it's gon'na catch up with you? You playing games. That ain't gon' fly, blood."

I rose to my feet and let characteristics of the old Khalid

come out. "What, nigga? You stupid in your head! I'm playing a game? Nigga I know the game and it ain't nuttin to play with! Fuck what you think Moseley! I'm the lucky one. Most of the people that I got started in the game with are dead. But my dumb ass lucked up and went to jail. Now I come out and see your ass going down the same path. But at the rate you're going, I don't think you'll be as lucky as me."

"Yeah, whatever, fuck what you saying," Moseley said. He began to search around the room for something.

"That's how you feel, Moseley?" I asked him. "Make sure you think about that."

"Fuck what you saying," Moseley said as he continued to search his room. He found a pair of pants and reached into the pocket. He pulled out a business card and handed it to me. "Give yo' big homie Boogie a call."

I looked at the card and saw Mr. Fix-It-All George "Boogie" Jamison with a contact number underneath it. "You wanna tell me a lil' bit more about this? Like where you get this?"

"Boogie himself," Moseley answered. "That nigga hooked Kush up with a gun and told me to give that to you."

I nodded my head even though there were so many other questions I wanted to ask. Too heated to stay in the setting, I left the room and retreated to the living room. I sat down in the love seat and slung my leg over the left arm. There were a thousand thoughts running through my head. I knew something like this would happen. This is how this game goes. It's always one down and more to go. Revenge thrives in some gangbangers. The need to seek revenge on enemies is so big that it will never die. First Jordan, then Derrick, maybe Moseley and Nyrique.

Moseley's meddling comment had me questioning myself. Maybe I was meddling because Kiani was involved in this. I knew this was so much more than that, even though she had ties to this situation.

Damn, I thought to myself, *is this situation out of my hands? Do I leave it alone and let it fade away over time? Or can I actually end this?*

No doubt about it, I'm fucking with fire. I can possibly get so involved in this that I actually get pulled back into the streets. I wasn't sure if this was my battle, but I was willing to do my part. I grabbed the phone and immediately dialed the person who knew everything going on in the hood: James Knightly, aka Nite.

When he answered the phone, his voice was sluggish and he almost sounded high off of weed. "Yoooooo, wasssssssup bloooood?" he dragged all three words.

"Nite? Is this you man?" I asked just to make sure. Once he verified it was him, I continued. "Yo', tell me what happened when y'all hit 30s up, blood." I acted like I knew it was them who did it for sure. If he went ahead and told me, I had my answer. If he didn't know what the hell I was talking about, then I still had my answer.

"You mean that dirt gang?" he asked dissing the crip gang.

"Yeah, them niggas," I replied.

"Oh blood, we went through they hood and hit dem niggas up. Got that nigga Nyrique and Derrick!" Nite answered as he relived the action that night they did in the drive-by. "Missed the other two mu'fuckas."

"For real! Who was in the car?" I asked with forced excitement.

"The usual affiliates. Me, Kush, Slim, and Mo," he answered. "Moseley didn't tell you, my nigga?"

"Some of it, but he had to go so he never finished the story," I lied.

"Yeah, that nigga Derrick's funeral was today. Shoulda

went through there and shot all them crabs payin' their respects," Nite said.

I cringed at his words. I said, "Well, you know that nigga Derrick wasn't even a gangbanger."

"So the fuck what, blood?" said a defensive Nite. "He was at the wrong place at the wrong time with the wrong niggas."

"Obviously. So now he pays the price?"

"Somebody's got to pay it. Now them dirt-gang niggas know not to fuck with 20s. That's a muthafuckin' message and if they want more—we got more."

"Oh really?"

"Yup," Nite replied. "That's how this shit is."

In a sad way, he was right. "All right Nite, I'll see you around," I said, ending the conversation now that I had my answer.

"Aight then, blood," Nite said before hanging up the phone.

I looked at Boogie's business card, which was still in the same hand that Moseley handed it to me in. *Maybe I should give Boogie a call*, I thought to myself. I had dodged the hood long enough, and eventually I was going to have to face the music. I didn't hesitate to dial the number. I waited calmly for someone to answer the phone.

"Hello?" the deep friendly voice answered. I knew it was Boogie.

"Boogie! What's up with you?" I asked. Now that I was on the phone with him, I was glad that I would be able to let him know where I stood with the hood.

"Who's this? Aw, don't tell me it's my lil' nigga Hide," Boogie chuckled. "Hey loc, what's good witcha?"

"I'm all right, man. Tryna stay outta jail, you feel me?" I casually replied.

"I know where you coming from, man," Boogie said.

"Tell me, though? Why you came over to the crib to say what's up face-to-face?"

I laughed uneasily and said, "Ah man . . . I don't know. Shit, I been working, though. My girl hooked me up with a job so that's where my focus is."

"Yeah, you gotta work to get ya paper nowadays," Boogie said. "I tell you what. I'm having a lil' barbecue over here at the house. C'mon through, man, say what's up to an OG." Boogie laughed that deep, hearty laugh that made me smile every time.

"All right bet! I'll be there," I answered. I would catch the bus over to the old neighborhood where I did my growing up and gangbanging.

I freshened up by taking a shower and throwing on a pair a basketball shorts, a white tee, and black converse. I stepped outside and noticed that Los Angeles was a totally different scene from what it was this morning. Earlier it was gloomy, cold, and raining. Now that the sun was shining brightly, the clouds had disappeared, and any evidence of rain had dried up. Southern California residents were dressing the part in short, tank tops, sandals, and sunglasses.

I made it to the bus stop just in time to see it pull up. I flashed the driver my bus pass and he nodded his head. I made my way to the back of the bus and sat in the empty backseat. The next stop, three young men got on. The first one was light-skinned with acne marks on both cheeks and braids down his back. The second was short, sporting a fade, and a nose ring. The third was tall, slender, and had a baseball cap pulled low over his eyes. They each paid their bus fare and mobbed to the back, all three eyeing me intensively.

"Where you from, my nigga?" the short one asked me.

I raised an eyebrow at that question. "I don't bang, homie."

"You don't bang?" asked his tall friend, standing up on his feet.

I stayed calm and seated. "That's what I said," I replied.

"Well, give up that chain, then," the six footer said. Shorty stood up, ready for what he thought was going to be a bus fight.

"Nigga, you ain't gettin' this chain," I said, grabbing the gold rope chain Kiani had given me as a gift.

"Hold up," the light-skinned male intervened. "None of that today. Nigga said he don't bang. Leave him alone."

The other two friends looked at him and took their seats. That made me smile on the inside. Things were totally different from when I banging. Anybody was getting jacked, whether you gangbanged or not. If you didn't have a hood to call your own, you were definitely targeted. Not nowadays . . . too much shit was going on for the innocent to be preyed on. I was grateful that the light-skin male had enough sense to calm his hotheaded friends down.

Once I arrived at my stop, I exit the back doors of the bus and walked three blocks down to Boogie's house. The same cars from back in the day were in the driveway. Memories instantly played themselves out before me. I pictured Boogie shooing Pablo, Rock, Aaron, and me off the hood of his '86 Camaro. He loved that car more than anything, and we loved to sit on the hood and blaze a joint.

Boogie often let us sip forty-ounce malt liquor on his front porch. He would always tell stories of how him and his buddies loved sipping on St. Ides.

In the tune of Snoop Dogg and Nate Dogg's St. Ides commercial, he would sing, "Just hit the corner store, you know what I'm looking for! St. Ides!" It was sure to come after he told one of his funny malt-liquor stories. When he and his friends were too young to buy liquor, they'd drive all across town to go find a liquor store were they weren't known just to steal a bottle.

I rang the doorbell once and was greeted by Boogie himself.

"Hide, lil' youngsta! Check you out! C'mon up in here," he said with a huge Kool-Aid smile on his face.

"What's good, Boogie?" I said laughing, which I couldn't help but do. Boogie hadn't changed a bit. He was still an OG with the build of a linebacker, but friendlier than a golden retriever puppy. Only when crossed would he transform into the thug that even his enemies didn't want drama with. I stepped into the house and shook his hand.

"Man, everybody is in the back gettin' down on that barbecue I just hooked up. And let me know you, that sauce ain't nuttin' to play with. Woody's Bar-B-Q ain't got nuttin' on me," Boogie bragged. "We can go on back there in a minute. C'mere right quick. Wanna show you sumthin."

Boogie led me to the powder-blue leather sofa in the living room, and boy was it a sofa to look at. I'd never seen a leather sofa in a powder-blue color, and I wasn't surprised that Boogie was the one to have it in his living room.

"Yo Boogie," I said, ready to crack a joke. "Where you get this sofa from, man?"

Boogie shook his head as if that wasn't the first time he was asked that question. "Man, don't even ask me. My wife wanted this piece of shit. You know Boogie don't get down with that blue . . . especially on a muthafuckin sofa," he chuckled.

"Oh, the wife wanted it, huh?" I laughed.

"Man, never mind this sofa. Check this shit out," Boogie said, placing a nugget of lime-green–colored kush in my hand. "Smell that, Hide."

I held the weed to my nose and almost coughed from the aroma. "Whoooo-weeee! Smell like some fire to me," I said, handing him the weed. "Who hooked you up with that?"

"A shotta of mine from Jamaica. You know they got that

good shit out there and somehow someway he brought it to Cali. Me purcheese nuttin' but da best mon," Boogie said in a Jamaican accent.

"Ah, that's cool," I said, though not so enthusiastic. I didn't smoke so I wasn't excited about the pure kush he was holding.

"He looking for somebody to sell it for him too," Boogie said. "You wanna get in on it?"

I shook my head and replied, "Nah, Boogie. I don't know if you heard or not but I ain't into all that no more."

Boogie was silent as he put the kush back in the Ziploc bag and wrapped the plastic bag up in a cloth. He put the weed into a jewelry box and said, "Nah, I heard. The tiny locs you used to run with back in the day been telling me. And I ran into your friend Mo, I think his name was."

"Yeah, he gave me your card," I told him. "Look, just keeping it real, I know I shoulda stopped by a long time ago to let you know something."

"What? That you done with gangbanging? Don't wanna be down with the hood no more?" Boogie said, looking me in my eye.

I didn't look away. Instead I looked him in the eye and said, "Yeah, Boogie. I went to jail and I finally got it when I got out. That ain't the life for me, you know? I'm doing things different this time. I told Pablo and them to tell you—"

"Yeah, they did," Boogie said, leaning back in the sofa. "But of course they claim you used other words."

"I just feel like the hood ain't my home no more. Nobody visited me in jail, none of them niggas from Van Ness. Not even you, Boogie. Wassup with that?" I asked him.

"Hold on, Hide. I asked your boys to give me your info. None of them niggas had it. They said you wasn't calling them or none of that," Boogie explained.

My face frowned up because I knew that was a lie. I

shook my head and said, "I tried to call one of them niggas damn near everyday. After two weeks of them not answering my calls and not writing me back, I just said fuck it."

"Well, why you ain't write your big homie? I wish I would have known," Boogie said, regretting that he didn't do enough to visit me. "I shoulda did my own search, hell."

We laughed at the situation and the circumstances.

"Those little niggas did me dirty," I said. "Ain't no way in hell I would ever trust Pablo, Rock or Aaron. I don't care if we did share the same hood."

"Well, even if you don't wanna be a thug no more," Boogie said genuinely, "you need to know that I'm always here for you. I love you like a son. I'm glad you tryna change. I wish you the best, Hide."

Had it been anyone else, I would've told them to call me Khalid. But Boogie, unlike some of my friends, recognized that I was trying to change and accepted it with open arms. He could call me Hide as long as he wanted and I wouldn't complain about it.

"Now let's go on in the backyard and get down on some Boogie's BBQ," he said, anticipating the barbecue he had put his heart and soul into.

"Sounds good to me," I said as I imagined how delicious the food was going to be now that I was on good terms with my big homie.

"Oh, and by the way, I was just testing yo' ass with the weed. Just wanted to make sure you was really focused on changing."

"Yeah, Boogie. Sure you were."

Chapter Twenty-six

Kiani

"Happy birthday to you, happy birthday to you, happy birthday Khalid, happy birthday to you!" my friends and family sang when I entered Danielle's living room.

Here it was, February 17, my birthday, and I was twenty-one years old. I was blessed to see this age. At the rate I was going a couple of years ago, I should've been dead. It felt good to be doing legal work, making hard-earned money, and in love. The first person I eyed when I walked in the door was Kiani. That was how things went now. In a sea of people, I noticed her first. I grabbed her face gently and kissed her cheek.

"Did you throw this for me?" I asked her as her cheeks turned a rosy red.

"It was me and Danielle's idea," she answered. "We've been planning this since the beginning of the month. But of course with the funeral there were some setbacks."

"You did fine. I know you had something to do with the decorations," I said as I eyed the Disney streamers, balloons, and party hats.

"I sure did," she said with a smirk. "You're twenty-one, but the little kid inside of you lives on." Kiani placed a party hat on top of my head and let the rubber-band string pop me under the chin.

"Ouch," I said drily.

She laughed at me as I took the hat off of my head and said, "Well, your guests love the decorations. Dior is actually planning on using them for her baby shower."

I kissed her cheek and told her I would be back. I found Moseley, Anthony, and Calvin in the kitchen sipping on red cups with who-knows-what in them. They didn't look happy, but didn't look sad either. They looked as if they did not want to be at the party, but came for the sake of me.

"Don't you all look happy," I said sarcastically.

They each looked at me, giving me the same awkward stare.

"Well, I'm not," Calvin replied.

"Obviously."

"Man, Dior is fucking pregnant. I don't know what the fuck I'm going to do. She's keeping it—acting like she doesn't know how this is going to change our damn lives! She got the nerve to be out there all happy and giddy! She acting like this shit ain't even happening!" Calvin said. "Nigga, I don't even know how I fuckin' feel! One minute I'm happy, the next I'm pissed. Shit!"

"I guess it's time for you to start saving up then," I suggested.

"Fuck that shit! I got fucking fired from my job. I don't know how I'm going to support a family with no job!" said a bitter Calvin. He downed the rest of the liquid in his cup.

"Sell drugs," suggested Moseley.

"Don't," I intervened, "sell drugs. That's stupid."

"You did it," Anthony said.

"And went to jail for it too," I said with an attitude.

"Nah, you just got caught. I'll make sure I won't get busted. Shit, what else can a nigga do?" Calvin asked, feeling that doing something illegal was the easiest way out.

"Rob a liquor store," Moseley said.

"Y'all niggas are stupid," I told them. I was so disgusted that I didn't even want to be around them.

"Ain't it funny how you want to call us stupid for attempting to do the same shit yo' ass did?" Calvin asked me.

"Ain't it funny how you're dumb ass won't get the hint? I'm tryna keep y'all from making the same mistake I made. Over and over again I see y'all about to make the same mistakes I made, and 'cuz I care about y'all niggas I'm lookin' out for you. I guess I was dumb enough to think you'd actually get the hint." I turned to walk away.

"Hypocrite-ass nigga," Calvin mumbled just loud enough for me to hear.

I didn't respond. I kept my back turned and left the kitchen. I found Dior and Shay engaging in a conversation in the hallway. Both were wearing party hats and seemed to be enjoying themselves. They spoke to me before I could speak to them.

"Hi Khalid!" they said gladsomely and in unison.

"Don't you guys look cute in your party hats," I replied, making a mockery of Kiani's idea to have party hats at a twenty-one-year-old man's birthday party. "Y'all enjoying yourselves?"

"Yeah, it reminds me of a two-year-old's party, but it's all good," Dior answered. "Whatever Kiani wants to do is her choice. Happy Birthday, Khalid."

"Thank you," I answered. I turned my eyes to Shay.

She gave me a hug and said, "Happy birthday boy."

I found it difficult to hug her back. "Thanks, Shay. How have you been?"

"Good, Khalid," she replied. "So what else are you doing for your birthday?"

I shrugged my shoulders and answered, "I don't know. I appreciate the little party Kiani threw for me. This is all I need."

Shay smirked and nodded her head. She looked at Dior, who acted oblivious to the situation. Shay looked up at me and said, "Well, this week I'll be in town. You should let me take you out to eat."

"So you want to take me on a date?" I assumed.

"No, I want to take you out as a friend. After all, we are friends, right?" Shay asked, somewhat mischievously.

I moved back two steps and placed my hand under my chin. "Something like that. Just call me. Excuse me, ladies," I said.

I went out the front door to retrieve my lighter from the car. I had a Black & Mild I wanted to blow away. Anger suddenly fumed inside me when I saw Kiani holding a conversation with Pablo, Rock, and Aaron. She knew the history I had with them.

"Kiani!" I yelled. She turned around gracefully, even though my outrageous tone might have came off frightful.

"Hey baby," she answered. She came over to me and wrapped her arms around my waist. "Look who showed up!"

"What the fuck are they doing here?" I asked low enough for only her to hear.

Kiani answered just as quietly, "I don't know. They said you had a talk with some guy names Boogie and y'all were cool now. I figured they heard about the party and decided to just stop by."

"Khalid, my nigga Hide!" said a fake smiling, Pablo. "How you been doing? Staying low-key?"

"Nigga, what the fuck do you think you're doing, blood?" I said as I let Hide who'd been balled up inside me come out.

"Simmer down, Hide," Rock laughed. "Boogie set us all

straight and told us not to fuck with you no more 'cuz you tryna do some good in your life. But we still ya niggas, right? Can't we be cordial? We got a present for you."

Aaron took a birthday card out of his pocket. "Happy fuckin' birthday, blood," he said in between short breaths.

Pablo and Rock hopped into the Dodge Charger they arrived in. Aaron squeezed his body into the backseat. They drove off, leaving both Kiani and me puzzled.

"Are you going to open it, Khalid?" Kiani asked.

I ripped open the envelope and took out the birthday card. On the cover was a picture of a gun plastered over a black piece of construction paper. I wanted to rip the home-made birthday card into pieces. But I was so surprised that they went through the trouble of making me a homemade birthday card and wanted to see what was inside.

"Open it up and read it, baby," Kiani insisted.

To satisfy her, I opened the card and read the "poem" written with a pen.

Happy Birthday Khalid aka Hide. We're really glad you're still alive. You got a lovely bitch on your arm hope you keep her away from harm. In order to do that you'll do your best. Don't you worry 'cuz soon there's a test and if you do good she will thank ya. Put on the hood once but always a gangsta.

Kiani's face flushed with a look of horror. Without saying a word, she turned around and went into the house. She must have known trouble was brewing between my old pals and me, and she was in the middle. I balled up the birthday card and threw it in the garbage can that sat on the curb. I followed her inside and saw her sitting on the sofa in a completely different mood from when I first came to the party. Her face made me draw a blank. For the first time I found it hard to read her mind.

"Kiani, that letter is bullshit. You know I'm not going to let anything happen to you," I comforted her.

"Bullshit? Well, for the past month everyone's been acting on what they said they're going to do," Kiani said. "That letter scared me, Khalid. It really did." She quivered.

"Baby, do you trust me?"

"Hell yes, I trust you."

"Then trust that I won't let anything happen to you. Give me that at least," I begged her.

Kiani's next words brought reality back into play. "I can do that but you're not Superman. You can't protect and serve everybody."

"What do you mean?" I asked for clarification.

"Aw, Khalid, you're so sweet," she sighed. "You're only human. You can't try to protect me and your friends and yourself from a world you think you know. Pretty soon you'll get dragged back into the same lifestyle you walked out of."

But that's just it, I thought. *Had I been protecting my friends better, then maybe this situation could have been avoided.*

"Like you told me at the funeral, it isn't your fault. Shit just happens. Unknown, coincidental, spontaneous. It just occurs. Who are we to try to stop it? We almost . . . we almost can't," Kiani continued, as if reading my thoughts.

Her last words echod in my head.

We almost can't . . .

We almost can't . . .

We almost can't . . .

Chapter Twenty-seven

Dior

Just when you think shit can't get any worse, it does, Calvin thought as he took long steps into the house. *I get fired from my damn job, I got a baby on the way, and my girl is on some crazy shit.*

Calvin entered the house and went straight into the bedroom. He opened his door to find Dior sleeping peacefully in his bed. He didn't want to wake her, but at the sound of the door closing she awoke.

"Hey baby," Dior greeted. "How was work?" She never gave him the chance to answer. "Oh, baby! I got to thinking. We should really get an apartment together. You think that's a good idea? I don't like the idea of us living here . . . in this room."

Calvin looked depressed as his girlfriend spoke of goals and dreams of being a complete family. He knew his surprise would totally shatter all she had to say.

"If I keep working and you keep working, we can save up," Dior suggested. "What do you think?"

Calvin sat down on the bed next to her and grabbed her

hands. "Baby, as lovely as all this sounds, right now it is a bit unattainable."

"Well, why is that?" Dior asked.

"I got fired from my job," Calvin spat it out loud and clear.

Dior's face grew tense, then softened, and she began to cry. "Really? Well, how? Why? And how are we supposed to support a baby with my little-ass income?"

Calvin shrugged his shoulders. "I don't know."

"You don't know? You don't know why you were fired?" Dior asked.

"I got caught smoking weed in the workroom," Calvin answered, feeling embarrassed by his answer.

"You got caught smoking weed, eh?" Dior asked sarcastically. "What a fool. How the fuck—no, why the fuck are you smoking weed at work? I could just scream right now!"

"Please don't," Calvin mumbled. He was already irritated with his pregnant girlfriend. "I don't want to talk about it."

"You don't want to talk about it? Well, we're going to. I'm involved now. Of all things to get fired for . . . you get caught smoking weed?" Dior rambled. "Calvin, how are we going to support this baby?"

"Dior, just shut the fuck up. I'll get another job, damn it!"

"Within the next three months, right?"

"What the hell are you putting a time limit on it for?"

"I'm six months pregnant, Calvin. In three months I'm due. That's why there's a time limit on this!"

"Dior, don't make this bigger than what it is. You need to chill and relax. I can get another job. Stop worrying yourself. I know my baby has a headache!" Calvin joked.

Dior sucked her teeth and replied, "Obviously, you don't find this as serious as it is. Good to know where your head is at."

In outrage, Calvin stood up and yelled, "See, that's why I can't come to you about shit. You're always thinking negatively about us!"

Dior was confused and begged to differ. "Calvin? What the hell are you talking about?"

"I don't want you here right now. Did you drive?" Calvin asked.

"You don't want me here? Are you serious? And yes, I did drive! You want me to leave?" Dior asked.

Calvin nodded his head. Dior was taken aback his request. "Fine, that's fine," she said as she grabbed her belongings. "And I sure hope to see your deadbeat, no-job-having-ass at the baby shower this week."

Calvin could've cursed her out for her name-calling, but it wasn't worth it. He truly wanted her out of this house. Dior marched through the living room and saw me on the sofa, looking up at the ceiling as if I was contemplating something.

"Khalid, if you find the real Calvin please let me know because whover that man is in there sure ain't my baby's father," she said before leaving the house.

Dior went toward her car while dialing up Kevin's number. Kevin answered on the second ring.

"Yo', wassup Dior?" he answered, excited that she actually called.

"Hey, are you busy?" Dior asked as she started the car. She hoped he'd said no.

"I'm not busy. Why? Did you want to come over?"

"Ah, you read my mind. So it's cool if I stop by?"

Once Kevin gave her the okay to come over, Dior sped out of the neighborhood and into the next one over. She was at Kevin's grandmother's house at what seemed like a moment's time. He must've heard her car screech in front of the house the way he damn near ran out of the front door. Like a gentleman, he opened the door and helped Dior out of the car.

"Jesus, Kevin. I'm just pregnant, not handicapped," Dior replied.

Kevin chuckled and responded, "It's good to see you, Dior."

"Good to see you too, Kevin," Dior said. "How have you been?"

Kevin held the front door open for her and answered, "I've been good. But what's more important is how you are doing."

Dior followed him to his room. She sat down on his bed that had been occupied by a female the night before. Dior took a deep breath and sighed. She had a sad look on her face. Kevin took notice.

"Go ahead and cry, Dior," he said.

"What?" Dior asked.

"I know that look. You want to cry, don't you?" Kevin asked. He sat down next to her and put his arms around her.

At that moment, Dior collapsed into tears. She sniffled, "Calvin and I got into an argument. He lost his job and I don't know how the hell we're going to support this baby. It seems to me that he's not taking it seriously. Kevin, I don't think he knows how important this is!" Dior felt good to know she had a shoulder to cry on, but she was skeptical about it being Kevin. "Or maybe he does but he isn't showing it."

"Well, I know how important this is," Kevin said as he grabbed her hand and caressed her shoulder.

Dior eyed him like he was up to no good, and he was. "Kevin—"

She was halted when he moved in to kiss her. She pushed him away and stood up. "Kevin, don't you ever try no sucka shit like that again!"

Kevin was confused. He said, "What the fuck, Dior? You told me y'all got into an argument."

"But that doesn't give you the right to try to move in on me! God damn!" she exclaimed. "Just like something you would do. It was wrong of me to come here."

"Sorry, I was confused," answered an irritated and embarrassed Kevin.

"I said we got into an argument. I never said anything about us breaking up. So what are you confused about, Kevin?" asked Dior.

Kevin rolled his eyes and responded, "Look, I said I'm sorry, damn it."

"Right, but don't try to take advantage of me. I may be vulnerable, but I'm not weak," Dior clarified. She made it certain that she was still Calvin's woman, regardless of the arguments and disagreements.

Kevin wore a blank expression. It was the look Dior could never read, but she knew he was sorry.

She softened up and said, "Okay, Kevin. I forgive you and I won't bring it up anymore. Okay?"

Kevin smiled, showing all pearly-white teeth and followed it with a laugh. Dior asked him what was so funny. "My look still puts you on the soft side. Obviously I still got it," he answered.

Dior frowned and replied, "Yeah, whatever. You may have that but I'll tell you what you don't have anymore."

"Ooh, that was fucked-up Dior."

"Give me the benefit of the doubt. I'm pregnant."

"Don't use that to your advantage," Kevin replied. "You're a good girl. I just wish I never fucked things up with you. But things always happen for a reason, right?"

"Not necessarily," Dior contradicted. "Shit just happens. That's life."

Chapter Twenty-eight

Calvin

Calvin walked into the soft pink-and-canary yellow–decorated living room. There was a sea of Dior's friends gathered there, some he knew and some he didn't. He froze when all eyes wandered on him. They were calling him father and dad-to-be. They named Dior mommy-to-be and rubbed her watermelon-shaped belly. She was seven months pregnant, smiling radiantly, and showing how excited she was about the baby. Calvin didn't register it yet. He was so confused. *How could she be so fucking happy about a baby that's going to slow us down?* Calvin thought as he made his way toward her. He kissed her on the cheek. Dior forced herself not to get angry. She played it off very well with an artificial grin.

"C'mon, you two! Let us get a picture of the parents!" shouted Dior's mother.

Whatever, Calvin thought, *that's the least I could do to thank you for throwing this stupid-ass baby shower at your house.* He and Dior posed for some pictures, both faking their happiness in different ways. Dior didn't like the thought of Calvin being so close to her because she was still disgusted by his recent behavior. Calvin just didn't want to be at the baby shower, but showed up for the sake of respect toward Dior and the baby.

Calvin and Dior sat down together, neither of them having much to say to the other. They answered questions from the guests.

"Have you thought of a name for the girl?"

"Not really, but we'll probably keep it in the designer theme," Dior answered.

We will? Calvin asked himself.

"Calvin, when are you and my daughter going to move in together?"

"No, better yet, when are you two going to wed?" asked Dior's overbearing aunt.

"Very soon, very soon. But I don't want to make it seem like I'm only marrying her because of the baby," Calvin responded. "Don't worry. I'll marry her when the time is right."

Good fucking answer, you jerk, Dior thought.

"Well, that's not good enough. Maybe you should have married her before you all got pregnant," said the loud-mouth aunt.

"Man, fuck this bullshit," Calvin cursed aloud, not caring about the ears he offended. He quickly exited the room.

"Auntie?!" Dior yelled, taking his defense. "That was just rude and uncalled for. You need to learn to keep your mouth shut!" She stood up and quickly chased after her man. She caught him walking toward his car. "Calvin, wait up!"

"What the fuck do you want, Dior?" he asked angrily.

"Please don't leave. Baby, where are you going?" she asked peacefully.

"Why do you care?"

"So you're going to leave our baby shower?"

"*Our* baby shower? Our? Dior, you're the one who's pregnant! Not me!"

"What the hell is your problem? You're acting like a bitch! Always running away from something. Face it, Calvin!" Dior said, fed up with her boyfriend's stubbornness.

"A bitch, Dior? Okay. I won't run away this time. Watch me walk away from you," Calvin said. He went to his car, started it up, and drove off.

At first he planned to let the streets lead him wherever, but he decided on going to Evan's house. Evan seemed to be the only person that wasn't working his nerves. He called him to inform him ahead of time that he was on his way over.

When he arrived, Evan was already waiting on the porch with his friend Mase. Evan and Mase made it to the car before Calvin even stopped.

"A yo', you ready to do this shit, man?" Evan asked.

Calvin shook his head and looked away from Evan and Mase. "I'm not feeling too good about it now," he said.

"Man, don't bitch out on me! You hood or not? Prove it. Winning fights and bangin' yo' hood don't make you no fuckin' G," Mase said. "You ain't a gangsta till you rob a mu'fucka. Shit, I'll kill a nigga if I have to. It's nothing to me. I just don't give a fuck." Mase laughed.

His words sent a chill through Calvin's body. "You sound like O-Dog from *Menace II Society*," Calvin said. "Dumb nigga."

"Nigga, I am O-Dog from *Menace II Society*. The Hughes Brothers got that nigga from me," joked Mase.

"Shut the fuck up. You ain't that old," Evan replied.

"I taught you how to be a gangsta. You put in work and got your stripes. We just gotta work on this punk nigga Calvin," Mase said.

"Nigga, shut the fuck up! Stop running yo' mouth. I ain't doin' this shit! If we get caught I can't go to jail. I got a baby on the way," Calvin told the two.

"Fine, we won't do it," Evan said. "All right Mase?"

"Cool," Mase replied. "We won't do it for the punk. Go to the liquor store so I can get a Swisher. I got some bud I wanna blow."

"Now that's a plan," Calvin said agreeing with smoking a blunt.

Calvin drove to the liquor store and opted to stay in the car as Evan and Mase went in. Unbeknownst to Calvin, the two boys were about to perform the robbery anyway. It played out like a movie. Mase went up to the front register.

"Let me get two grape Swishers," he demanded.

The cashier turned his back and out of nowhere Mase hopped over the counter and began to beat him maliciously. Evan, meanwhile, went in the back for any additional cash. Mase pumped two deadly shots into the store owner's head. He took the money from the cash register and found additional cash in the dead man's pockets.

"C'mon Evan. I got the money. Let's get the fuck out of here!" Mase said.

"Aight cool," Evan said.

Evan and Mase ran out the store and hopped into the car. Calvin, who heard the gunshots, was confused.

"What the fuck did you do? You just robbed the liquor store?" he asked.

"Man, shut your bitch ass up crying! I should smoke you too!" Mase held the gun toward Calvin.

"Nigga, get that gun out my fuckin' face!" Calvin yelled.

Evan broke the two up. "C'mon you two. We gotta get the fuck outta here! Drive!"

The three were so busy arguing they didn't notice the police vehicle pull into the lot. The two police officers got out and walked into the liquor store. Calvin was first to spot it.

"You gotta be fuckin' kidding me!" he said, wondering to himself just how long the policemen had been in the store. "Why, God? Why me?" He quickly started the car up, but didn't have enough time to drive off without being noticed.

"Get out of the car!" the policeman yelled with his gun in hand.

Calvin panicked, put the car in drive, and attempted to drive off. Instead he ended up driving into a light pole. The air bags popped out of the dashboard and steering wheel, smacking Calvin and Mase in the face.

"Shit, nigga! What the fuck! You can't drive now?" Mase yelled.

Evan groaned painfully. He was thrown into the window, thankfully not through it. He was bleeding on his head. "My fuckin' head hurts!"

"No shit! You're bleeding like a muthafucka!" Mase replied angrily. "This is the last time I rob a store with Calvin's stupid ass behind the wheel."

"Mase, I'm going to tell you for the last time. Shut the fuck up," said Calvin. Though his voice was calm, he spoke with a firmness that let Mase know he was not in the mood.

The policemen called for backup and demanded that they get out of the car. Calvin, Evan, and Mase got out of the car and put their hands behind their heads. They were each handcuffed and put in the backseat of the police car. At that moment Calvin realized he was going to jail and faced the possibility of receiving the charges for a crime Mase and Evan committed.

They were taken to the police station, interrogated, beat up by the officers, and then sent to jail. Later that night, Calvin was allowed to phone Dior.

It was around eleven at night when she heard the phone ring. Calvin's bed seemed so empty without him and therefore she could not sleep well. Dior answered her ringing cell phone with the unknown number.

"Hello?" she answered.

"This is a collect call from the California Correctional Facility. Calvin—"

Dior immediately accepted the charges. "Baby! Oh my God! What happened?" She feared the worst just knowing the call was coming from jail.

"Mase and Evan robbed a store and I was with them," he answered shamefully.

"You're kidding."

"I'm calling you from jail so I'm not kidding," Calvin said. "Damn, baby. I fucked up! At first we were planning to do it, but then I said I didn't want to do it. I took these niggas to the liquor store and they end up robbing it anyway."

"It turned deadly?" Dior asked.

"Mase shot the store owner twice," Calvin replied.

"Why were you planning to rob a liquor store in the first place?" Dior asked.

"To get some money for you and the baby," Calvin admitted.

"What was wrong with you just getting a damn job? That was so stupid." Dior made it clear that it was very unwise of Calvin to stoop so low as to planning to rob a liquor store.

Calvin already knew this. He didn't need Dior to constantly remind him. "I know that Dior. But what you fail to realize is that I said no. I wasn't going to do it. Evan and Mase did it, and I was driving. So now it makes me seem like I'm a part of it. But I swear that had no fuckin' idea!"

"My Lord, Calvin. How much is your bail?"

"Seventeen hundred."

"Calvin, where am I going to get seventeen hundred dollars?"

"Savings, Dior!"

"We don't have that much in our savings yet! And on top of that, the savings account is for our daughter. I can't do that!"

"I'll replace it!"

"How? By robbing another store?"

"Fuck you, Dior! You know what? I don't need you. I'd rather be here in jail than with you."

"Cal—"

He hung up.

"Shit!" cursed Dior. She knew she was at fault for using sarcasm at the wrong time. There was no need to be rude to Calvin since this day— the same day of his baby girl's baby shower— would be a day he would always regret. She immediately called someone who she hoped could come through in a way that seemed impossible.

Shay answered her cell phone on the fourth ring. "Hey, Dior. What's the problem?"

"Girl, Calvin is in jail and his bail is seventeen hundred dollars. Now that's money I just do not have at all!" Dior said.

Shay sighed helplessly and said, "Damn, girl. I don't get paid until next week. I don't have seventeen hundred on me. Hell, I don't even have seventeen hundred dollars in my account."

"Fuck!" exclaimed Dior. "I'm stressing myself out so much I might fuck around and go into premature labor."

"You better be careful, girl. Take it easy, please go easy," Shay replied. "I got an idea."

"What is it?"

"Kevin. For some reason he's the kind of guy who always has cash on him," Shay said. She knew it was because Kevin had a large amount of money stashed away prior to him going to jail, and retrieved the stash when he was released.

"Kevin? I can't ask him for that money! What do I look like?"

"Like a girl in need of some help," Shay answered. "Swallow your pride and ask that man. You can pay him back."

"Shay, I can't—"

"Dior, I don't wanna hear no more. I told you what to do," Shay said. "You better handle that. Now can I get back to bed?"

Dior replied, "All right, you can."

"Sorry I don't have the money."

"It's all right. Thanks anyway."

Dior hung up with Shay and scrolled through her phone and called Kevin's recently added number.

"Yo wassup," Kevin answered his phone as if it wasn't eleven-thirty at night.

"Kevin! Bad news. Terrible news, in fact," Dior answered.

"What happened and what do you need?" Kevin asked in response.

Dior was hesitant, but her request eventually came out. "Calvin is in jail for some bullshit and his bail is seventeen hundred dollars, money I just don't have right now," she swiftly replied.

He had heard every word. "All right. I got you. Come on over and get it," Kevin answered.

Dressed in just how she was, pajamas and house slippers, Dior grabbed the keys to her car and drove to Kevin's house. When she arrived, he met her on the porch.

She put her hands together as if she was praying to him.

"Kevin, I swear, you are my hero!" Dior admitted. "Thank you sooooo much. You came through in a way so big I can't even tell it."

"It's nothing," he said.

"I can pay you back at the end of the month, I promise."

"Don't worry about it. You don't have to pay me back," Kevin replied. "You just hold onto that money and take care of that baby, promise?"

"I promise," Dior said, grabbing him in a hug. "Thank you so much, Kevin!"

"You're welcome," Kevin said smiling. He knew that the reason he was giving the money to Dior without asking for her to pay him back was from their past. Dior had accepted him for who he was long before he went astray and got locked up in jail. This was his way of saying thank-you. She taught him that it was okay to not roll with the in crowd and it was better to be your own person. Had he been smarter in his decision-making, he would not have gotten involved with gangs and drugs. That was the biggest mistake he ever made, because that cost him his relationship with Dior. A monetary gift would help ease some of the guilt he felt for making that mistake.

"All right, all right, but once again, thanks a lot, Kevin," Dior thanked him once more.

"Will you just go get your man?"

Dior did just that. When Calvin was released, he ran into Dior's arms and gave her the tightest hug.

"Damn, baby," he sighed. "You came through."

More like Kevin did, Dior thought.

"You used the money from the savings?"

I could have used the money from our savings, but that would've set us back, Dior thought. The only thing that mattered to Dior was her baby and her man. *And Kevin doesn't want me to pay him back? This is my blessing in dis-*

guise. She received the bail money without having to be in debt to another, and her family savings went untouched.

"Hey," Calvin said, snapping Dior out of her thoughts. "Did you use the money from the savings?"

Dior nodded her head in reply to Calvin's question. That was a lie, but with the way things were going, throwing fuel in the fire would result in an explosion.

Chapter Twenty-nine

Kevin

"You did what?" Nyrique asked.

"I gave her the money to bail Calvin out," Kevin replied.

Nyrique shook his head at this. Information like that was something he'd be too embarrassed to tell his boys. "Ain't this about a bitch," Nyrique replied. "And ain't you being one! What nigga in his right mind would give a bitch money to bail *her boyfriend* out of jail?"

"A nigga like me," Kevin chuckled. "You know how I feel about Dior, man."

"You're being a trick," Nyrique spat.

"It ain't tricking if you got it."

"So where the hell did you come up with seventeen hundred off the back?" Nyrique asked.

"Man," Kevin said slowly. "When I was doing my thing before I got locked up, I had about forty grand stacked up."

"Forty fuckin' gees? Kevin, stop lying," Nyrique interjected.

"Shut the fuck up and let me tell the story. Now I had

forty gees stashed when I went to jail. My sister, the only woman I trust, held the money for me. Now that I'm out, that should be enough to get me by for the next year or so."

"More like months. You know how we blow cash," corrected Nyrique.

"All right then months," Kevin replied. "So it was nothing to give Dior seventeen hundred dollars. She doesn't even have to pay me back."

Nyrique laughed at him hysterically. "You head over heels over this girl."

"Shit, I might be. That's my baby," Kevin admitted. He had no shame and would broadcast it to the world if he had to.

Nyrique made all efforts to remind him that Dior was Calvin's lady, and was now pregnant with his child. Kevin was going to play himself if he made any more passes at Dior. "I hope you didn't think this was a way to get to her. Paying her nigga's bail? Of all the things . . . that dumb shit surprises me the most," Nyrique said. "You gon' blow this kush with me or not?"

"Count me out. I gotta have a clean system for my PO, man," Kevin said. "Holla at me when you're done."

"Cool, I'll be at Bee's house," Nyrique said before he exited the room.

A palm-tree leaf fell on his front lawn from the gust of the March wind. Kevin was almost blown over too as he watched the trees sway to and fro with every blow of the wind. Litter from the trash cans blew in the street and onto the yards of homes. Just like the wind, Kevin's thoughts were whirling every which way.

Kevin questioned himself on if he should have told Nyrqiue what he did for Dior. Now he felt stupid after being ridiculed by his friend. But knowing it was for Dior put him at ease. He decided to call her.

Her phone rang twice and the person who answered certainly was not Dior. Seeing Kevin's name on the screen and knowing that was the name of Dior's ex-boyfriend did not sit well with Calvin when he saw her phone vibrating at the end of the bed. She was in the shower washing away cum and sweat from the sex session they had moments ago. Calvin took the liberty of answering the cell, and felt obligated being that it was Kevin's name under a blinking incoming call.

"Who the fuck is this?"

"Kevin."

"Kevin who?"

"Kevin, Dior's friend," he answered calmly. This threw Calvin off guard. "Who is this?"

"Calvin, muthafucka."

"Calvin who just got bailed out of jail?"

"Yeah, nigga. What the fuck you doin' calling my phone?" His nostrils flared with anger. His clenched fist pounded against the mattress. He felt like steam would burst out of his ears . . . all because another man was calling his girlfriend's phone.

"Your phone? Last I recalled this was Dior's phone," Kevin replied.

Calvin snapped back, "My bitch, my phone!"

"Hold up, homie. Don't come at me sideways. If I were you, I'd be nice to me," Kevin chuckled.

This only angered Calvin more. "And why the fuck is that?" He made no effort to tone down on the language.

"Where do you think she got the money to bail yo' no-good ass out?" Kevin asked.

"Oh, for real, nigga? Get the fuck off my phone with that shit, blood!" Calvin demanded.

An angry Calvin threw Dior's phone at the wall, smashing it into broken pieces. He stormed into the bathroom and pulled back the shower curtain, revealing a nude and fully pregnant Dior. She gasped and damn near jumped out of her soapy skin.

"Calvin, baby, you scared me," Dior laughed. She became uneasy when noticing the stern look on his face.

He solemnly asked her to step out of the shower. The power in his voice, although he spoke softly, was apparent to Dior. She turned the shower faucet off and wrapped a towel around her body. She followed Calvin into the bedroom. The wind from the ceiling fan gave her wet body a chill.

"I'm going to ask you this one time and one time only," he said as calmly as he could. "Where did you get the seventeen hundred dollars from?"

Fear crept into Dior. She looked around helplessly, as if she would find the answer somewhere in the room, but Kevin wasn't there with them. She noticed her phone had been thrown into the wall and split into pieces. She knew Calvin had figured out her dirty little secret.

"Answer me right now," he barked.

"Kevin gave it to me," Dior said quickly. She flinched, thinking Calvin was going to slap the shit out of her.

Instead he did something strange and unusual. Calvin was the one to leave this time. He left without uttering a sound, putting Dior in a puzzle and wondering where their relationship was heading next.

But later that night he returned, ready to confront the issue. Though he was high and drunk, Dior still decided to have a talk with Calvin. He turned off the television she was watching, commanding her full attention.

"I'm really mad at you for not telling me that you got that money from Kevin," Calvin began.

"I am so sorry. I didn't want to touch the money we had set aside for the baby. Kevin gave it to me when I asked him," Dior apologized.

"Oh, I know that now," Calvin replied. "But what did you do to get the money?"

"What? What do you mean, what did I do? I asked him for it, Calvin," Dior answered.

"You didn't do any favors?"

"Hell no! Calvin, what kind of girl do you think I am?"

"Well, I know how oral friendly you are," Calvin spat.

"That was just cold-blooded," Dior gasped. "How can you say something like that? I should have left your ass rotting in jail."

"You could never do that," Calvin laughed.

Dior was flustered with anger. "Oh really?" she asked, surprised by his happy response. "And why is that?"

" 'cuz you love me." Calvin then cradled on top of her and kissed her neck.

Dior cringed with desire. Now she couldn't even stay mad at him and she hated that. She tried to resist, and found her reason to. "You smell like weed and liquor. Get off me."

"C'mon, baby. Stop playing. Let's just get over this. I love you and you love me and you're having my baby."

Dior questioned if this was Calvin's voice or if the weed and liquor were talking.

"Oh, yeah," Calvin said as if he had forgot something and remembered it. "You can't talk to Kevin anymore."

"What?" Dior asked. First Shay, and now it was her turn to be told to end a friendship with an ex-boyfriend.

"I know it ain't gon'na be a problem, right?" Calvin asked her.

"How can I just x the person who bailed you out of jail for me out of my life?"

Dior asked.

"Are you serious? I can't believe you would ask me a question like that? I'd rather you had let me stay in jail than you get the money from your ex-boyfriend! You can't x him out now? He's your x-boyfriend— of course you can ex him out the picture!"

"Calvin, you're taking it the wrong way," Dior defended. "He didn't ask for no favors, and I didn't offer none."

"No, I'm taking it just how you said it! It seems to me like you want to keep Kevin around," Calvin said.

Dior shook her head frantically. "No, no, no, no, no, Calvin," she pleaded. "That's not it, I swear."

"Well, I'm going to make this *really* simple," Calvin concluded, exaggerating the really. "It's either Kevin or me. So choose wisely."

"Calvin, you already know it's you."

"Then I'd suggest you start acting like it. From here on out, Kevin is done."

Chapter Thirty

Anthony

Anthony threw the book of his designs on the couch. He had just finished drawing a design for the jeans he hoped to create. Earnestly, he had been working with a fashion-design teacher in college on clothes for a university runway show. It was a big deal for Anthony, career-wise. Local LA designers, celebrities, and boutique owners would be attending the event.

Anthony would take his drawings to his teacher, Mrs. Bailey, who would present them to the fashion-show coordinator in hopes of getting him in the show. This was all to take place at three o'clock today.

When the time arrived, Anthony met Mrs. Bailey in her classroom at the university.

"Hey, Mrs. Bailey," Anthony greeted her.

"Hello, Anthony. How are you doing, sweetheart?" she joyfully asked.

"I'm good, a little nervous, though," Anthony admitted. He held a tight grip on his book of fashion sketches.

"Well, why is that?" Mrs. Bailey asked.

"I just hope my designs are good enough to land me a spot in that runway show," he replied.

Mrs. Bailey said, "Ah, yes! About the designs. Good news or bad news first?"

Anthony frowned. All he hoped for was good news, but opted to hear the bad news first.

"All right," Mrs. Bailey said. "Well, as for the fashion show . . . you're out."

Anthony breathed heavily and composed his anger. He asked why the decision was made when he had not even submitted his work.

"That's where the good news comes in," Mrs. Bailey said smiling. "I did a little something. I'm good friends with a fashion designer in New York . . . Manhattan, to be exact. I submitted your previous work to her and she demanded that you go to New York to work with her as an intern."

The fashion designer who wanted Anthony on her team was Antonia Capponi. She was a New Yorker with a heavy accent and was proud to be Italian. She was on the verge of creating her Capponi line of mens and women's wear, Italian, inspired clothing meshed with the styles of urban wear.

"You're kidding!" Anthony did not believe it.

"No, I'm not! It's the opportunity of a lifetime. This is your dream, right? I'd take this internship if I were you. You'll be getting paid as well!" Mrs. Bailey said. She was so excited that one would think she got the deal. "So what do you say?"

"What can I say? Of course I'm accepting the offer! Damn, thanks so much, Mrs. Bailey!" Anthony gladly said and reached for her in a hug.

"No problem! Anthony, you're a fashion genius and I expect great things from you and Lady Capponi," Mrs. Bailey told him. "I gave her your e-mail address, so expect an e-mail from her very soon."

"I will, I will," Anthony said.

He had hit a grand slam. Not only was he going to be living in the one of the fashion capitals of the world, but he would be living his dream of becoming a fashion designer there as well. He was eternally grateful that this opportunity came along and there was nothing or no one that would stop him from going through with it.

Chapter Thirty-one

Shay

I thought that I was over Shay, being that the love I had developed for Kiani was so real and powerful. But when Shay called that gloomy and rainy April evening, I got excited. I hadn't heard from her since my birthday and was starting to think I finally had gotten rid of my Shay problem. But I didn't get rid of her that easily.

"Khalid. What's up?" Shay asked.

"I'm good. Haven't heard from you in a minute. It's been like a month or two?" I asked her, hoping to make her feel bad.

"More like three. I saw you in February on your birthday. It's the middle of April," Shay said jokingly.

"Well, you've been hella busy," I told her.

"School, finals and all. I've been dedicating my time to that," Shay replied. "And you, Khalid? You haven't called me. What or *who* has been taking up all of your time?"

Shay thought she was slick. But I'd play right along with her. "My girl Kiani takes up most of my time. I work for her father so I see her just about every day," I answered.

"Charming," Shay replied drily. "Well, I miss seeing you."

"Miss seeing you too," I answered.

"Well, we could put an end to the missing. Can I see you tonight?" She asked.

"You're going to come over here?" I wanted to know what she had in mind.

Shay responded, "I'll come over there to pick you up and we'll go out to eat."

"You want to go out to eat?" I asked, surprised. "With me?"

"Why are you surprised, Khalid?" Shay asked.

"Because you actually are suggesting this," I answered. "It's coming from your mouth . . . not mine." I made no hesitation to tell her why I was shocked that she wanted to hang out with me.

She defended herself by saying she had always wanted to spend time, with me but she had recognized I was serious about Kiani and decided to back away for a little bit. "I didn't know if you were taking this girl seriously, but I guess you are."

"Yeah, I am," I answered proudly.

"So, can we do this, Khalid?" Shay asked persistently. "I won't take no for an answer."

"So then I have to say yes," I said.

"Basically," Shay giggled.

"All right then," I said reluctantly. "So what time should I be ready?"

"You need to be ready by seven," Shay replied. "I'll honk when I'm outside."

"All right, I'll be ready," I agreed.

"Okay, see you then."

Shay and I got off of the phone. Almost immediately after I got off of the phone, it rang again.

The name on the caller ID read *WESLEY*. It was Kiani.

"Hello?" I answered when I picked up the phone.

"Hi baby. How ya been?" I never got the chance to answer. She continued, "Well, tonight my family is having game night. I wanted you to come. I can come pick you up around seven."

Damn, how convenient, I thought. *Now what do I say?*

"Aw baby," I moaned. "I already have plans."

"Oh . . . well, where are you going?"

"I'm going to a dinner party for the homie, babe. I'm sorry."

"Oh, it's okay. Have fun tonight, okay?" she said. "Bye baby.

Getting off the phone with her hurt like hell. This was the first time I had lied to Kiani and it did not feel good. How can people lie to the ones they love when it hurts like this? I answered my own question. It would hurt Kiani even more if I told her the truth. Not that that made it right. I knew what I had to do.

I decided to call back. She answered the phone as if expecting my call.

"Yes, Khalid?"

"Kiani, I wasn't honest with you," I began.

She cleared her throat.

I continued, "Actually, Shay had asked me to go to dinner with her. I kind of agreed to go."

"You *kind of* agreed or you did agree?" Kiani asked for clarification.

"I said I would go."

"Aw, baby," Kiani said upset. "All I ask from you is honesty. I know you can do it because you've done it before. Why lie now?"

"I know, that was stupid."

"That was a real question."

"Oh," I said. "It involved Shay, so I didn't want to start any drama in our relationship."

"Khalid, I'm not worried about Shay. I trust you around her," Kiani answered. "It's her I don't trust. But then again, she's not the one I'm in a relationship with."

That was good to know. Kiani had grown so much in our relationship and I saw her growth more and more each day. I couldn't let a little white lie stunt that growth. In many ways I felt like I had earned Kiani's heart and I was determined to keep it.

"But you not telling me the truth first time around makes me worry," Kiani said.

That was a good point. I couldn't help but agree. I apologized to her for lying. She accepted it, but it seemed forced.

"All right, but call me when you get in," Kiani said before hanging up.

I breathed a sigh of relief. I felt good after telling the truth, and felt even better that Kiani was understanding about it all.

When seven o'clock arrived, I was definitely happy to see Shay and even more happy that my girlfriend knew about it. Just as she said she would be, Shay was in her car honking away. When she saw me nearing the car, she ceased. I got into the passenger seat and sighed.

"So where to?" I asked.

"I hope you're up for some Mississippi soul food," Shay laughed.

"Always ready for some M and M's!" I said. My stomach was yearning for the soul food I had yet to taste.

Shay drove off speedily, but once we hit the main street she got ridiculously slow. I told her that she drove like an old lady. She replied that she wasn't going to ruin Dior's car. No one wants to get yelled at by an eight-months-pregnant woman. Not to mention the drama with Calvin was taking a toll on her.

"I sure hope everything goes okay with Calvin and

Dior," Shay said. "His court date is set for next month on the twenty-eighth. Hopefully he won't miss out on the birth of his daughter."

"It doesn't look too good," I said, giving my honest opinion. "He fucked-up big-time."

"That he did."

I hoped for a pleasant dinner and conversation at M and M's soul food restaurant. One part of the expectation was fulfilled, but the conversation went haywire.

"So what happened to us?" Shay asked.

"Are you serious? Why are you asking me that question?" I asked. I took a sip of my lemonade—very sweet and very much a black thing.

"Because I want to know. It just seemed like all of a sudden, we grew apart. Maybe it was when Kiani came around," Shay replied before tasting my lemonade over her Coke.

I shook my head. "No, it definitely wasn't that. It all started because of you. You were wishy-washy and never for sure. Nyrique sure as hell didn't help. You told me you couldn't talk to me because of him. Kiani had already been in the picture before that, but I was feeling you more back then."

"And now?" she edged on.

"Now I like you, but I love Kiani. Straight up," I answered.

"The thug has gon' soft," Shay noticed.

I was only this way with Kiani and Shay. That was no mystery.

"Well, damn," Shay snapped. "Khalid, I tried to make peace with you after that."

"But I was with Kiani . . . and I still am! It doesn't work like that. You can't run in and out when you feel like it," I told her.

"I know that, Khalid. Believe me! I just feel bad about it all. All I want to do is right my wrong."

"So you take me out to dinner?"

"It's a start," Shay said grinning.

I looked away. Shay talked a good game, but I wasn't falling for it.

"So if you'd allow me to do something I should have done a long time ago—

"What the hell is that?" I interjected.

"Khalid," Shay began. "I want to have sex with you."

Her words echod. *Sex with you . . . sex with you . . . sex with you*. She had to be kidding. But she didn't crack a smile. *Well damn.*

"Look, I know it may be wrong. But this will be the first and last time. You know you want to."

True.

"We have to do it sometime."

True.

"Kiani won't have to find out."

Uh-oh.

"The secret is safe with me."

"And Nyrique? This nigga already thinks I killed his homeboy and now I fucked his girl."

"What about him? I haven't heard from him since he got locked up."

"Locked up? For what?" Damn, it seemed no one was safe from jail.

"He beat up this old man and went to jail for assault and battery. Two years."

Well, I guess that handles Moseley's problem for the next two years. "Oh, so you feel it's only right you fuck with me?"

"*You* feel it's only right."

True . . . no wait! Fuck!

"Let's go," Shay said authoritatively.

Those two words alone put me in a trance. Her tone was so sensual and demanding. The next thing I knew Shay and I were in the hotel room together. This girl was down and it turned me on . . . all the way on. I was so on while lying on my back with Shay on top of me, kissing my neck. The hotel bed was king-sized, the room was dark and Kiani was nowhere in sight. Shay tugged at my belt.

"C'mon, Khalid. Let's do this," she moaned.

Oh shit. This girl wants it so bad, and something deep inside me just told me I can't.

"Shay, no," I said. I gently removed her from on top of me. "I can't do this, sweetie. I love my girl too much."

"Khalid, are you serious? Obviously, you don't love her enough. You're in this hotel room with me," she hissed.

"Obviously, I don't like you enough because I'm not going through with this. I'm leaving, Shay. I'm sorry," I replied.

"Where are you going?" she yelled viciously.

"Home. I'll catch the bus."

"You got me fucked up, Khalid!"

I walked out of the hotel room, pride and all. I was upset with myself for even letting it get this far. Worst of all, this was something I had to tell Kiani. It would only be right of me to do so. She deserved to know that I messed up, and if she could find it in her heart to forgive me and move on, then I'd be fine. But I refused to have what just happened between Shay and me bothering during my relationship with Kiani. I was a firm believer that what you do in the dark comes to the light. Therefore, it was better that I tell Kiani before she found out in another way.

Chapter Thirty-two

Kiani

As the April rain beat against the windowpane, I watched her engage in a game of Scrabble with my little cousin. Abdullah was an outside child who enjoyed backyard games of basketball and soccer, especially with Kiani. But thanks to the showers that came with the month of April, he was forced to play board games inside the house. Kiani had 284 points from three well-defined words already. Her cousin had a score of 32 points from the words *CAT*, *CHECK* and *MET*. Kiani seemed to enjoy beating the child Abdullah in Scrabble in a playful way while extending his vocabulary at the same time. When she would spell a word out on the board, Abdullah would ask what it meant. Kiani, who carried an extensive vocabulary, would give him the answer every time.

I only hoped to God the sadness I was feeling was not depicted on my face. She damn sure hadn't noticed. Every time she looked at me, she smiled . . . and I forced myself to give her a grin in return. I fucked-up big-time and I knew it.

"Kiani," I said once I gained the strength to talk to her. "Follow me into the bedroom."

"Um, baby," she said, nodding her head toward my little cousin. "Not right now. I'm playing with Abdullah."

"It's okay. I know what sex is. I heard it feels good," cousin Abdullah said. He knew too much for his own good.

"Watch your mouth," I told him. I turned my attention toward Kiani. "It's not about that. It's something important."

"Okay," Kiani said, then she looked at Abdullah. "Can you hold on a minute, please?"

Abdullah nodded and watched Kiani and me go into Danielle's guest bedroom.

"This really does have something to do with sex, right?" Kiani asked with a wistful expression on her face.

I shook my head and answered, "It's about last night."

Kiani's facial expressions shifted from yearn to concern. I knew I had her full attention by the way she sat on the edge of the bed, eyes focused on me the whole time. She appeared brokenhearted already. Knowing that I was the cause of this made me sick to my stomach. I was about to unleash a demon.

"Shay and I went to dinner," I began. I took what seemed like the longest pause of my life. The lump in my throat finally dropped and allowed me to say, "And we went to a hotel afterwards."

Kiani folded her arms across her chest as tears began to creep from her eyes. Her leg shook, almost uncontrollably. It was her way of releasing her anger. She shook her head as if she didn't believe me. She angrily replied, "Why'd you stop? What the fuck happened next, Khalid?"

"We started kissing-"

"Did you fuck her?"

Kiani had never cursed in my presence. To hear her

curse—and cursing at me—was surprising. The reaction only got worse.

"No, I didn't fuck her. We were about to, but I got up and left," I explained.

"I don't believe you!" Kiani screamed.

"Wait a minute! And please stop yelling," I replied. "I swear, Kiani, I didn't fuck Shay! You can ask her yourself!"

"Why the hell would I ask Shay? So she could lie to me too? Whose dumb-ass idea was it to go to the hotel anyway?" Kiani asked.

"It was hers."

"Bullshit."

"No, it's not bullshit."

"So it was Shay's idea?"

"Yes it was, baby."

"Why did you decide to go?"

"It was a mistake."

"Answer the question."

"I just did!"

"*It was a mistake* is not an acceptable answer and neither is *I just did*!" sobbed Kiani.

Exhausted, I exhaled and loudly sighed. Now I didn't know what to say and I had no idea where the conversation was going. This was when I let go of the reins and let things run free.

"Answer the muthafucking question!" Kiani yelled.

"Now wait a minute! You not gon' get away with yelling at me like you're crazy."

"I'm not crazy! I'm pissed!" she cried. "I don't get black guys! A girl can give you her money, her mind, body and soul and you still won't be satisfied! Khalid, I've given you my all, everything and more . . . yet you still are not satisfied!"

"No, that's not true. I love you, girl. Swear, I've never felt like this about another female in my life . . . and probably never will if you leave me. I've learned to love with you. You gotta believe me."

"So what's the deal with Shay? Do you still have feelings for her?" Kiani asked. It hurt her to have another conversation like this, moreover to bring Shay back into the mix of our relationship.

"I thought I did. But being in that hotel made me realize just how much I wanna be with you," I answered.

"Oh really? So you mean to tell me that I was on your mind while you were kissing that bitch?" Kiani asked. "You keep saying all the wrong shit."

I shook my head. "Hear me out baby—"

Kiani interrupted me. "I've heard you out before. After that time she told you she loved you, I heard you. You said she was nothing. *It was a fling from back in the day. Those days are over, Kiani.* Remember that, Khalid? Bullshit! Lies! You end up in a hotel with this bitch and you want me to hear you out again? What do you have to say this time?"

"I couldn't even go any farther with Shay because my relationship with you means more to me than she ever will. That doesn't right the wrong I did in going to the hotel with her, but at least I was man enough to walk out."

"That's bullshit," she mumbled. Kiani tried to hold her composure, but her emotions got the best of her sending her into a collapse. She cried her tears, cursed me out, and fell to the floor. Kiani looked distraught and hurt. It irked me to know I was successful in hurting the first girl I ever loved. I lifted her off of the floor and held her in my arms, rocked her from side to side, hoping to take away much of the pain I caused her.

"I'm sorry," I whispered in her ear as a tear escaped from my eyes. I had never cried over a girl. It had to be love, being that I was standing here crying with Kiani.

"Yeah," she said, snatching away. "So am I." She walked

out of the room and made sure to give Abdullah a hug good-bye before she left the house.

As she walked down the street to her car, she noticed two young males walking toward her. They seemed to have come out nowhere, but Kiani wasn't focusing her attention on them. She was so out of her element after hearing about last night's secrets.

When she neared them, she looked up and noticed it was Pablo and Rock. Kiani stopped dead in her tracks, and turned around to run back to the house, but it was a second too late. Pablo and Rock grabbed her. One covered her mouth and the other wrestled with her hands. They took her into the last house on the block, Rock's brother's house.

Kiani begged for them to let her go. She thought they were going to kill her. But little did she know they had other ideas in mind. She bribed them with money, her car, and even food. Nothing seemed to work. She wished someone could come to her rescue, but help was nowhere in sight.

Pablo put the blindfold over Kiani's eyes and tied her arms up with what seemed like a leather rope, preparing her for her undoing. Kiani tried to break free, but it didn't work. All she could do was stay still on the bed, screaming with pain as Pablo and Rock took turns beating her until she passed out.

Chapter Thirty-three

Dior

"Girl! I got something to tell you!" Shay exclaimed. She burst into the bedroom and handed Dior her keys. "First of all—is Khalid here?"

"Nah, he went to Danielle's house. What happened?" Dior asked, sitting up in the bed, already attentive to what Shay had to say.

"Girl, so you know I went out Khalid's stupid ass last night," Shay began her story. Just by her adjectives like stupid, Dior knew the date wasn't what Shay expected. "Well, after we ate, we went to hotel."

"A hotel?" Dior asked. "Shay, what the fuck. You know he goes with Kiani."

"But Khalid and I have a past. I just wanted to close that chapter," Shay explained.

"Chapter? Past? Khalid is your past for a reason! You decided that you were going to close the Khalid case by sleeping with him?" Dior asked.

"Well, it's a first time for everything," Shay said.

Dior groused, "Shay, I am so pissed off at you, it's not even funny. Number one, that's disrespectful to Kiani. That sweet girl? She did nothing to you, but you decided all of a sudden you wanna sleep with her man."

Shay rolled her eyes at the comment, upset that her best friend was angry with her and she hadn't heard the whole story. She wasn't in the mood to be condemned. She had already been played by her ex-admirer. Getting scolded would only intensify her anger.

"How could you, girl?" Dior continued.

"Well, don't get your panties in a bunch," Shay mumbled. She admitted, "Khalid didn't even fuck me. He ended up leaving me dry in that hotel room. He said he couldn't do it."

Dior shook her head disapprovingly. "That's a good guy. He was able to walk away from that? 'Cuz I'm quite sure you were ready to put it on him!"

"Shut up," Shay commanded. "I'm very mad because I ended up looking stupid!"

"Well, that's what you get! Never try to push up on somebody else's man, first of all. Second of all—"

"Don't start, Dior. I thought I was talking to my best friend, not my mother!" Shay said.

"Don't let Nyrique find out. He'll have your ass beat from behind bars," Dior joked, though what she said was highly likely.

"The only person I told was you so if it gets out that's me on your pregnant ass!" Shay said.

Dior shrugged and said, "Oh, don't trip. This shit is safe with me. No doubt. But I'd like to talk to o'boy."

"Who, Khalid? Ugh!" Shay stuck her tongue out and pointed to it.

"I want to know why he even went to that hotel with you. Why did he put himself in that position anyway?"

"Oh, so you don't blame me?"

"Girl, I blame the both of y'all. You more than him because I know it was your idea to go to a damn hotel."

"Yeah, it was."

"Bad girl."

Dior grabbed her bag and headed toward the door.

"Where are you going?" Shay asked as she gathered her things. Dior walking toward the door was her cue to leave.

"I have to pick Calvin up from his mother's house. She insisted they have prayer for his trial," Dior said. "I made him go."

"Why didn't you go?"

"Didn't have to. I'm not the one that robbed a store. But I told them to pray for me," Dior said.

Shay nodded her head. "What did you ask them to pray about for you?"

"My strength," Dior answered. "My strength in my relationship, my strength as a mother, but most importantly, my strength in the Lord."

"Amen to that," Shay replied. "Well, call me when you get in. Are you enjoying time away from school being pregnant?"

"I don't enjoy being pregnant, but time out of school is cool. But I gotta go this week for finals."

Shay was escorted to the front door by Dior. Shay asked her if she could drop her around the corner at her aunt's house. Dior did just that.

Dior played her anger off with a smile, but she was truly upset and disappointed with her best friend. Now she wanted to hear the other side of the story. She had twenty minutes to pick Calvin up. That was enough time for her to talk to the second party.

She called Danielle's house. Danielle answered the phone and came into the room, handing it to Khalid before stepping out.

"Hello?" answered Khalid, all depression obvious in his voice.

"Khalid. You sound miserable. Let me guess . . . you told

Kiani about your rendezvous with Shay?" Dior asked, already knowing the deal.

"Sheeeit. Yeah, she's done with me, man," he answered sadly. "How do you know?"

"Shay is my best friend, Khalid. Did you forget?" Dior asked.

"Oh yeah," Khalid said.

"And you sound miserable, so I put two and two together. You two fucked up. I'm upset with Shay and pissed off at you," Dior said.

She was coming off annoying, but Khalid know she was only concerned about him. He gave her the benefit of the doubt and stayed on the phone with her.

"Khalid, why did you go to the hotel room with her?"

Khalid shook his head, not that Dior could see. But that was all he could do. He didn't have an answer for anything at the moment. The only thing on his mind was his good girl, Kiani, and how he messed their relationship up.

"You've got some major work to do if you want to keep her. You know that, right?" Dior mentioned.

Khalid already knew that. It was no mystery. The phone beeped, indicating another call was coming in. "Dior, there's another call coming in. I'll call you back," he said, preparing to click over.

"Oh, don't bother. I have to go get Calvin. See you at the house," Dior rushed.

Khalid clicked over and answered with his pleasant hello. It was Kiani. She was crying.

"Baby?" he said as part of him got excited from hearing her. "Baby? I'm sorry, Kiani. Don't cry, girl."

Kiani sobbed and slowly replied, "No, Khalid. It's not that."

"Well, what is it?" Khalid asked as he sat up.

"Pablo . . . and Rock."

Khalid's blood boiled at the mention of their names

coming out of Kiani's mouth. "Who?" he said to make sure he heard her right.

"Pablo and Rock. They beat me," she trembled. "They beat me, Khalid."

Suddenly, Khalid's sense of right and wrong went haywire. The only right thing to do was to protect Kiani and handle Pablo and Rock. He didn't care what happened in the end.

Chapter Thirty-four

Anthony

The party was an unexpected event in itself, but the secret that it came with was a real shocker. When a person found out Anthony was throwing a party, they expected a big bash. This was the first party Anthony had thrown in a long time and people were excited and expected one of the best events in the month of April. But they realized two things: This was no major party and the only guests were Anthony's family members and closest friends.

Dior and Calvin were first to express it to Anthony.

"A yo' Ant!" Calvin called as he pulled Anthony to the side. "This ain't the type of party people were expecting."

Anthony nodded and grinned. "Oh I know, man. This is a little different. But it will all make sense in a minute."

"Well, I'm glad it's like this. I wouldn't want people to look at me strange for bringing my pregnant ass to the party," Dior joked.

Anthony hugged her and rubbed her belly. The baby kicked and Dior laughed as excitement came over Anthony's face.

"What?" Calvin asked, noticing both Dior and Anthony's facial expressions.

"The baby kicked!" Dior said.

"I felt it! That's crazy, man! She responded to my touch," Anthony said.

Calvin took it as bragging and got envious. He tried not to let it show. He wished he had that bond already formed between Dior and the baby. Calvin had never taken the time to rub Dior's belly. He had missed out on ultrasounds, appointments, and other pregnancy milestones. He did not want his days during the pregnancy to be a reflection of the post-pregnancy days. He knew he had to step his efforts up and decided to start now. He instantly felt the sensation of being a father. He grabbed Dior and kissed her on the lips.

She blushed and asked, "Aw, what was that for?"

"For having my baby."

She was now red all over. Anthony took notice and left the two alone. He moved over to Shay and Moseley, who, oddly enough, were discussing Nyrique.

"Yeah, that boy is in jail for the next two years for assaulting this old man. And they had an issue before! I told Nyrique to leave that old man alone. They got into an argument and the old man called him a 'no-good son of a bitch,'" Shay informed.

"Damn, and he fired on that nigga?" Moseley asked.

Shay nodded. Moseley just chuckled and laughed. "That old man must've been near death if Nyrique got two years in jail," he said.

Anthony interrupted, "Hey y'all. Y'all doing all right?"

"Yeah, we're cool," Moseley answered on behalf of the two.

"Speak for yourself," Shay said. "Man, I thought this was going to be a party par-tay!" She snapped her fingers and did a little dance.

"Well, you'll find out why it's like this in a little bit," Anthony said. "But have any of you seen Khalid and Kiani?"

Shay rolled her eyes. She looked at Moseley and said, "Well, I don't know where he's at, nor do I care."

"Damn, what's your problem?" Moseley asked.

"I want to wait for him to get here, but he's an hour late and this isn't even his party!" Anthony said. "He has thirty minutes."

Thirty minutes went by and there was still no sign of Khalid and Kiani. Anthony could no longer wait. His guest had already helped themselves to the alcohol that was supposed to be opened up after he revealed his surprise. A few guests were a couple of sips away from being drunk.

Anthony gathered the guests' attention with a loud "Excuse me!" All eyes were on him. With the exception of a sidebar, the floor was his.

"All right, if you hadn't noticed, I only invited my family and close friends to this party," he began. "There's a reason for that."

Anthony took a long pause before he broke the news. "I'll be leaving for New York next weekend."

The room was now full of rumpus. They were all confused and demanded to know why.

"I got a really good job opportunity to work with a fashion designer, who also is going to pay my way through college. How could I not go?" Anthony explained himself.

Shay was the first to give a positive reaction. "Well, I'm happy for you, Ant. Congrats, sweetie!"

The other guests followed her lead and applauded. Any opportunity to succeed should be taken. That's exactly what Anthony did.

"So, we should expect to see your line of clothing within the next year, right?" Dior asked as she embraced Anthony in a hug.

"No doubt. I'll design an outfit for your baby," he said. "Promise you."

"Damn, why are you leaving so soon?" Calvin asked as he shook hands with Anthony as if he was leaving tonight.

"Originally, I was supposed to leave in the beginning of the summer. But Lady Capponi recruited me and this hottie to work for her as interns. The job starts a week after I get out there," Anthony answered.

"Hottie, eh?" Calvin laughed.

"Yeah, she's a mixed chick from Panorama City. I met her and she's real nice. So we'll be leaving together."

Calvin nodded and said, "Next thing you know you'll be her boyfriend."

"Playa for life," Anthony stated.

"Or until you meet the right woman," Calvin rebutted. He pulled Dior into him.

"How cute," Anthony joked. "But this is my career on the line. I'm focused, man." He certainly was.

Two hours later, the party was over and Khalid was just showing up. He spotted Anthony packing up some of his belongings. "Hey, wassup man. Where are you going?" he asked, plopping his body on the couch.

"If you were at the party you would know why," Anthony answered.

"Oh yeah, man, sorry I couldn't make it," Khalid answered. "Something came up with Kiani so I was at her apartment taking care of her." He didn't want to reveal any details.

"Kiani, how convenient," was the sarcastic reply.

"What's that supposed to mean?" Khalid asked.

"You missed out on the going-away party 'cuz you were out with some girl," Anthony told him.

"Now hold up, Ant. Kiani just ain't some chick. That's my girlfriend. And what going-away party? Who's going where?" Khalid was extremely confused at this point.

"I'm moving to New York. I got the opportunity to work with a fashion designer so I'm taking it," Anthony answered rudely.

"Damn," was the shocked reply. "That's good. Real good. When do you leave?"

"Next week," Anthony answered.

"So soon?"

"Well, you know some shit can't wait. Just wished you could have been at the party. But I understand your agenda." Anthony was still being sarcastic, and it was striking a bad vibe with Khalid.

"Anthony, you don't understand."

He interrupted Khalid, "No, I do understand. I do really. You'd rather be with Kiani than your homies."

Khalid cracked and spilled the bitter details. "No, Kiani got beat up really bad, Anthony! That's why I was with her. She was so damn traumatized and I've been with her for the past two days," he answered, letting the gist of his troubles be revealed.

Anthony stared at his distraught friend for a couple of seconds. It was a blank stare. It seemed as if he was trying to find the words to say. He finally decided on, "Damn it, Khalid. My bad. I'm sorry that happened. Who did it? Does she know?"

"It was Pablo and Rock. They snatched her up when she was leaving Danielle's house. To make shit worse, before that happened I had to tell her what went down between me and Shay."

"You did something with Shay?" Anthony asked.

I was so absent minded with all the drama going on, I had forgot that Anthony didn't know of my failed rendezvous with Shay. I felt obligated to tell him.

"After we went out to eat, we went to a hotel room. We was supposed to get it on but I couldn't even go through with it, man. I shouldn't have been in the hotel room with her ass anyway. It was my fault for even letting it go that far," he answered.

"So what are you going to do about Pablo and Rock?" Anthony inquired.

I bobbed my head. "I want to get them niggas so bad it hurts. But I ain't tryna get arrested."

"What makes you think you will get arrested, Khalid?"

"Because I'm gon'" try to kill their asses! Somebody is going to have to call the cops . . . and the paramedics. Man, if it were up to me I'd just kill them. Those niggas crossed the line."

"Handle that, then!"

"Man, I can't! That's what's pissing me off the most," Khalid answered. He decided to change the subject. "I'm going to miss you, Ant. Now who's gon'na dress me up for parties?"

"Just take my training with you, young grasshopper," Anthony laughed.

Khalid smiled at him. He was indeed happy for Anthony, for finding his ticket out of the hood and snatching it. I applauded him for it. That was the hood dream: To get out and be successful. Anthony achieved it. Now all he could do was hope he could get my dream fulfilled without going back to jail or being put in my grave.

Chapter Thirty-five

Kiani

Thursday was the only day it had not rained this week. Kiani and I took advantage of this as we walked down her neighborhood street. It was certainly a different scene in Culver City than it was in the area I lived in Los Angeles. There was a palm tree in front of every large home, along with a fancy car in the driveway. The sidewalks looked new and the streets were clean. Kiani lived in a safe neighborhood, and I began to ask myself if now was the time to move in with her.

She had not said anything since we started our walk. I gripped her hand tightly and pulled her body into mine.

"You all right?" I asked.

"I'm all right," Kiani said, refusing to look at me. "But I need a favor from you."

"What is it you need?"

Kiani had a change of heart. "Never mind, I won't ask you."

"C'mon, baby," I said, hoping that she would change her mind again. "Don't be scared to ask me. You know you can come to me about anything."

"All right, well lets get back to the apartment," she said.

We turned around and proceeded back to the apartment complex. I followed through the apartment's gates and to the front door. She unlocked all three locks; two of them she had installed after the event with Pablo and Rock. Kiani closed her door and locked the three locks, something she didn't used to do until now. It was part of her post-traumatic behavior. She placed her house keys on the dresser in her room. We proceeded into her bedroom.

"Are you going to tell me now?" I asked her.

Kiani answered, "Okay, Khalid. You love me, right?"

"Of course I do," I answered, thinking this was going into the Shay situation. "And I'm glad you chose to forgive me." Though I felt the beat-down from my enemies influenced her decision greatly, Kiani gave me the second chance and I appreciated it.

"This doesn't have anything to do with you and Shay," Kiani said. "It's about Pablo and Rock."

The hairs on the back of my neck stood up at the mention of their names. I could only imagine where this conversation was going.

"Khalid, they can't get way with what they did," Kiani said.

"Go to the police," I said.

Kiani shook her head. "Fuck the police!" she yelled. Those were two words I never thought I'd hear her say. "I want you to handle this shit!"

I pointed to myself. "Me? Why me?"

" 'cuz you're my boyfriend and I know you could do it! It's payback time, baby."

"Is that what the world is built on nowadays? Revenge? Kiani, have you forgotten—"

"Khalid, how could you not get back at them? That's like allowing them to do that shit. It's like holding me down with my legs open telling them to c'mon in and join the party!"

"C'mon Kiani, it's not like that. Don't exaggerate."

"You're just asking for it to happen again!" Kiani said, throwing her hands up in the air. "They even threatened this shit beforehand. Remember that shitty birthday card they gave you? They warned you, Khalid. They warned us. They're probably laughing it up right now."

"Kiani, what happened to you saying that I can't protect you? Where'd that shit happens stuff go now?"

Kiani rebutted, "Whatever happened to you saying you won't let anything happen to me? Baby, I don't feel safe going outside anymore. My God, I can't even drive past that neighborhood without getting scared. You aren't going to do anything about this, Khalid?"

"What you expect me to do?"

"What do I want you to do. I want you to kill them," Kiani answered.

My heart sank. I didn't know what to say to her. Kiani knew I would do absolutely anything for her, but she was asking me to kill—something that could end my life if it got traced back to me. What Kiani didn't fully realize was that I was a changed person. I didn't want to return to anything that reminded me of my old ways. Asking me to kill someone was a huge step back into that lifestyle. Even I had thoughts about killing Pablo and Rock, but I knew I couldn't do that. That wasn't the kind of person I was anymore. Let alone any opportunity the cops got to link me to something, they would take it. I'd be back in jail.

"Kiani, you can't ask me to kill them," I replied slowly.

"Why not? You love me, right?" Kiani asked ready to cry.

"Hell yeah, I love you," I said as I stood up and grabbed her hands. "But I can't kill anybody. Man, what if the police find out it was me? Then what? I go to jail for the rest of my life. I'm not doing it."

Kiani was quiet for a couple of seconds and then said, "Why are you so worried about the fucking police? You know they don't do any investigations in the hood. They don't care if y'all niggas live or die. They'd rather niggas be dead anyway. Makes their job easier. Shit! Any other man would take up for his girl! Kill or fight! You probably too scared to do that, huh? You wouldn't even fight them for me!"

I angrily pulled away from Kiani. What she said was out of line, disrespectful, and unbelievable to hear coming from her mouth. "Why are you talking like that? You sound crazy. You need to shut your mouth right now," I demanded angrily.

Kiani looked me up and down. "So I guess that's a no," she said.

I nodded my head and replied, "Hell yeah, that's a no!"

"Damn, Khalid. Look, you've made it this far in life. Shit, you know you can get away with it. You know you can!" Kiani exclaimed. "If done the right way, you could get away with it."

"What makes you so sure?" I asked.

"Khalid, look at what your name means. It means *immortal*. You think that came by chance? You've got away with your shit. And don't tell me you haven't killed someone before! So what, you went to jail a couple of times, but at least you still alive. You've lived your life like a cat with nine lives. Ain't you still hood?"

"What?" I asked, looking at her like the foolish girl she sounded like. I had never revealed to Kiani that I had murdered someone and had yet to be pinned for it. For her to assume that and bring it up to me in order to try to get her way was making me look at her in a different light.

"Hood! A thug! I know the old Khalid is down there somewhere. He ain't too far down that you can't get him out. If there was anytime you needed to go back to him, this is it! You seriously aren't going to take up for me?"

"Just cause my name means *immortal* doesn't mean I am, Kiani," I said, bewildered at what she was saying.

"That wasn't my point," she snapped.

"Well, my point is if I get caught, I'm going to jail for life!"

"And my point is," Kiani began, "make it so you don't get caught."

Chapter Thirty-six

Nyrique

TJ and Mike were sitting on Kevin's front porch. The two were sharing a thick blunt stuffed with California chronic. Kevin watched them get high and wished he could get high as well. With a probation officer from hell, he couldn't grant that wish.

"Damn, I can't believe that old man put my nigga Nyrique in jail. That's some bullshit. I ought to kill that mu'fucka," TJ said.

"Fuck that. He old as hell. He only got a couple more years left anyway," Mike laughed.

"Well, with the way y'all niggas bang y'all only got a couple of more years left too," Kevin said, telling the honest truth.

Mike and TJ simultaneously flashed him the middle finger.

"I'm waiting on a call from Nyrique too. Shay called me and told me he had some words for me," Mike said.

"Shay, huh? She still fuck with 'cuz behind bars?" Kevin asked.

"Sheeit, that's what Nyrique wants to think. He told me

and TJ to keep an eye on that bitch. Keep her from fucking with other niggas," Mike said.

Kevin knew Shay was going to find a way to talk to other guys regardless of the eyes she had watching her. Any female would risk it if she was truly ready to move on.

"You still tryna fuck with her friend, Dior?" TJ asked.

"That pregnant girl? Tell him what you did, Kevin," Mike said.

Kevin shook his head with a nervous grin on his face. He wouldn't speak.

"Well, if you don't tell, I sure will," Mike volunteered. "This nigga paid her baby daddy's bail. Seventeen hundred off the back, TJ! No questions asked!"

"Ah, you need to be shot for that one," TJ laughed.

"Well, her nigga told her she couldn't talk to me. And you know what? That's all cool. She got a baby by him anyway. I can fall back and let them do them. I ain't gon' try to force something that won't fit. But she knows I got her back if she really needs me. So, me and her are cool," Kevin explained.

"You sound like a bitch," Mike said, making fun of him. "You got used by your ex, and then played to the left."

Kevin's house phone rang. "Fuck all y'all," he mumbled as he went into the house. He answered the phone. "Hello?"

It was Nyrique calling from behind bars. Kevin accepted the charges.

"What's up, Nyrique?" Kevin asked.

"Shit, not a damn thing. I'm looking for Mike. You seen him, man?" Nyrique asked.

"He outside, hold on," Kevin said. He covered the receiver of the phone. "Mike! Ay Mike!"

Mike passed the blunt to TJ and went into the living room where Kevin was holding the phone. Mike took the phone from him.

"Hello?" Mike asked.

"Where the fuck you been, 'cuz?" Nyrique asked

"Why, nigga?"

"I called your house."

"I'm on the block, nigga, posted up at Kevin's. What's new?"

"Shit, I heard this nigga up in here from Van Ness Gangsters talkin' 'bout he glad that Derrick is dead. He said he wished all of 30s crips would get knocked off 'cuz we some weak-ass bitches. So when I stepped up and banged on his ass, he came at me with some Van Ness Gangster bullshit. Them niggas from VG killed Derrick. I know that for a fact now."

"Ah for real. It's on now! They be posted at the liquor store on Arlington and Fifty-fourth."

"Hell yeah, take my car and hit them niggas up."

"Oh fo sho. It's already done. I'ma get the other homies to ride. Hit me up tomorrow."

"Make sure your ass is at home, muthafucka!" Nyrique said before he hung up.

Mike hung up and told TJ and Kevin about the news. TJ was down to take action, but Kevin said he would think about it. Mike then called up other 30s crips members, who insisted they'd be ready around nine.

Just like that, the 30s crips and Van Ness Gangsters were even bigger enemies.

Chapter Thirty-seven

Khalid

With Calvin already in hot water from the robbery and Anthony already in New York, my choice was ultimately narrowed down to gangsta Mo to do the hit with me. Moseley was down with the plan before I even went into detail.

"Hell yeah, blood. Let's hit them niggas up!" Moseley laughed.

"Shit, man. I'm only doing this because they put hands on Kiani. That's the only reason! I'm not even suppose to be near a gun . . . and now I'm about to kill some mu'-fuckas. Damn it, man," I expressed my anger verbally. "I'm so to' up over this, Mo."

"It sounds like you're punking out," Moseley answered.

"Nah, I just don't want this shit to come back to me," I answered honestly. "It seems like my life is riding on this."

"Nigga, just act like how you used to be back in the day. You don't give a fuck! You wasn't trippin' on getting caught. Nine times out of ten you didn't—well, seven times out of ten," Moseley joked.

"Shut up, Moseley," I said rudely.

"Look, man, either you're gonna do this or you ain't. Make up your mind right now," Moseley said, giving me the ultimatum. "'cuz I got other shit to take care of."

Ain't this a bitch! This nigga getting on me, I thought. "All right, I'm gonna do it," I said.

"Sheeeit! How you gon' try to back out of the plan *you* told me about? You slippin'. I'm calling the homies Kush and Slim. You know them boys always down to kill a nigga," Moseley informed.

I nodded my head and began to think about the plan that was to be performed. It was going down like this: We would roll up to the liquor store on Arlington and Fifthy-fourth. If Pablo and Rock were there (most likely they would be), we would park and roll up on'em, empty some lead into them and shake the spot. Of course it wouldn't be that easy. Pablo, Rock, and their other affiliates would probably pull out their heat and strike back. Nobody wants to go down without a fight. Kill or be killed, straight up.

Moseley returned to the living room with the news that Kush and Slim would be joining us. Part of me was comforted, but still the other half was nervous. In a couple of hours, I was about to engage in the same activity I had condemned my friends for getting involved in. For many reasons, I wasn't so amped to do so. I never thought I'd be willing to do something like this. Instead of thinking about the jeopardy of my freedom, I was focused on the bruises I saw on Kiani's face and body. No one deserves to get away with malice like that . . . and I was going to punish the boys that felt it was okay to put their hands on my girl.

Nine o'clock came too soon. One minute I'm discussing this with Kiani and showing my rejection, and the next minute I'm embarking on it.

Moseley, Kush, and Slim were hyped about it. They had the music on full blast and bobbed their heads to the sound of the bass booming in the trunk. I should have known they were comfortable. To them, it's just another night. For me, it's life or death.

"Showtime, muthafuckas!" Kush laughed.

"You ready, Hide?" Slim asked.

I nodded my head. I look straight down Fifty-four.

"There it is," Moseley said, pointing to the boys standing in front of the liquor store. "Park this muthafucka!" He tapped Slim on the shoulder. "Time me. One minute," he joked.

Slim parked the car and looked at his watch. "Aight. One minute, starts now, blood."

Kush, Moseley, and I hopped out the car, guns hidden underneath our clothes and swiftly walked toward the liquor store. Sure enough, there was Pablo, Rock, and two other unknown faces. They made eye contact with us and like that it was on.

First the fight came. Punches were being thrown left and right. With every blow I gave to Pablo, I used even more strength. I was angry beyond words and I wanted him to feel it. Pablo pulled a bitch move and ran into his car, locking the doors. I started banging on the window . . . needing to hurt him some more before taking his life.

"You gon' lock the door, nigga?" I asked in a rage. "Open the fuckin' door!" I slammed my gun against the window, trying to break it open.

"C'mon man, calm down, man," Pablo said.

"Calm down? Calm down, nigga?" I asked angrily. "Fuck you!" I pointed my gun at his face, ready to shoot his ass through the window.

"I'm sorry, blood. I'm sorry."

I didn't believe what I was hearing. "You sorry? Damn right you sorry!" My finger grasped the trigger.

"Khalid, man! You ain't even gotta go this far!"

Funny how people come around when they see their life could be over. I took a sigh of relief, knowing deep down he was right. It didn't have to go this far.

Suddenly, the sound of gunshots rang out into the air, scaring the shit out of me. I didn't know who they hit. But once I turned back to Pablo, I knew. Blood was splattered against the cracked window with a bullet hole in it. I looked into the street and noticed Nyrique's old car. This had to have been Derrick's friends, TJ, Mike, and others from 30s crips.

I ran back to our car, hoping Moseley and Kush would follow my lead if they were smart. Sure enough, they did. We took off in our car, fleeing the scene.

"Damn! Van Ness got it good. Who do you think that was?" Slim asked.

"30s," I answered.

"Oh shit. I guess our job is done," Moseley said. "Let's get the fuck out of here!"

Though I didn't have to kill anybody, it still didn't justify death.

Regardless of who did it, death and violence were nothing to fuck with. I realized that all over again. It wasn't me who did the shooting, but I was damn sure about to. Thus, I still felt guilty.

"Yo' drop me off at Kiani's parents' house in Baldwin Hills," I demanded. "Now." Kiani was staying there for the night and I promised her that I'd be at her door after all was said and done.

"All right muthafucka, shit!"said an aggravated Moseley. "You ain't gotta get all mad at us."

They drove into Baldwin Hills, generating uneasy stares from rich, middle-aged black folks that the ghetto considered sellouts and the young, fly, and flashy offspring that lucked up with the wealthy parents.

"Young rich muthafuckas! I say we blast they young asses right now," laughed Slim.

"I can't stand these rich, sadity bitches from Baldwin Hills. I don't know how Khalid can fuck with one," Kush answered.

"Man, shut the fuck up," I defended. "Because I'd rather be in these rich folks' shoes any day than living in the hood."

"Well fuck you too! Get out the car," Moseley joked, as we pulled up in front of Kiani's house.

"Whatever, man. So what are y'all going to do?" I asked after opening the door but still staying in the car.

"Why do you care?" Slim asked.

Moseley answered on their behalf. "I don't know. Probably get some weed or drink—get fucked up."

"Well, whatever you do just be careful," I said as I got out of the car.

"Aight, man," Moseley said.

As they drove off, I shook my head at Moseley's transformation from the *wanna be a gangsta* to the *gon'na be dead before twenty-five*. He had developed that nigga mentality of don't give-a-fuck. As long as he lived that way, he would die the same.

Now depressed, I rang the doorbell. Kiani came to the door, opened it, and pulled me into a hug.

"Oh baby, I was starting to get worried. I hadn't heard from you. Did you do it?" she asked, leading me to her old bedroom. She locked the door behind her.

"I didn't have to," I answered. "30s already took care of it. TJ, Mike, and some other niggas."

"How do you figure?"

"They were in Nyrique's car."

"You saw it?"

"Yeah, Pablo got shot right in front of me," I replied. "Right before I was supposed to . . . kill him."

Kiani's jaw dropped. "Whoa," was all she could say.

I nodded in agreement with her surprise. "Crazy, huh? Why did they go after Van Ness?"

The mystery was unsolved. What were 30s crips doing hitting up Van Ness? Other than being crips and bloods, they had no direct beef. Kiani, being friends with TJ and Mike, gave TJ a call. "Hey, TJ. Heard you all went after Van Ness Gangsters."

"How the hell you find that out, rich girl?" TJ joked.

"Boy, I'm like the reporter. I always know the business," Kiani played along. "What was that about?"

"Nyrique got into it with a Van Ness Gangster in jail after he heard him talking about 30s and Derrick."

"What did he say?" Kiani asked.

"Talkin' some bullshit like he glad Derrick is dead and all the niggas from 30s need to get shot," TJ answered. "So we figured it was Van Ness Gangsters that shot at us at the park that one night."

"Wow," Kiani gasped.

"Let me hit you back." TJ ended the phone call.

Kiani informed me of the 30s motive. She immediately burst into tears and buried her face in her hands. I asked her why she was crying.

"I shouldn't have asked you to do that," she said. "That was selfish and low. The fact that you were willing to risk everything you have for me is crazy. And I love you for that, Khalid."

"It wasn't easy agreeing. I'm glad I didn't have to go through with it. But damn, I really was going to do that shit, huh? And it's better that I have this conversation with you now," I began. "I lied to myself when I agreed to kill them for you. I really made a terrible mistake . . . all out of love. We both realize that it could be me out there dead with Pablo, right?"

Kiani nodded her head and remained silent.

I continued, "What hurts the most in the end is that I had made a change, and made a commitment with myself to not go back into that shit. I don't know if you took me seriously."

"I'm sorry," Kiani whispered. "I am." The look on her face told me she felt guilty.

"Let me finish," I replied. "I'm not mad at you. I'm more upset with myself because I actually agreed to do it. This is the first time I've been in love and I see it'll make you do some crazy shit."

We laughed softly, knowing that love influenced a lot of our decisions.

I went on, "But I said all that to say this. I'm not Hide anymore. I don't wanna be, don't need to be. I want to be Khalid . . . and just that. And anybody that's in my life is going to need to realize that. Including you. I just want your word that you won't ever come at me the way you did when you asked me to do that favor."

Without any hesitation, Kiani stated, "I promise, baby, that I'll never ask you to do anything you don't want to do. I'll never come at you like that again, I promise."

A gentle kiss to my lips sealed her promise.

"It's a miracle that you came out of this alive," Kiani said. "And you didn't have to kill anyone."

I still felt bad about what I did to Pablo. I knew I would never be able to erase the look on his face as he begged and apologized to me. Deep down in my heart, I told myself to forgive him but I couldn't bring my lips to speak the words. "Yeah, I just can't believe 30s came around at the same time." Talk about an intervention.

It wasn't new to me to hear about gangbangers talking shit behind bars and it reaching the ear of the streets. In fact, it only confirmed my theory of Los Angeles being the big little city. Anybody knows somebody that knows everybody. People interact, cross paths, and meet. The only thing that makes this ten times worse is being in a gang.

The streets of Los Angeles were not terrible. We have our good neighborhoods and our healthy communities. But like every city, there is this underworld. The underworld is infested with gangs, drugs, violence, and sexual exploitation. It's easy to get into, but hard to get out of.

I'm fortunate enough to have made all efforts to get out of it. Though my battle isn't fully won, I'm almost to the mark. I'll always have my past as Hide, but it damn sure won't be my present or future.

"I love you so much, Khalid. I do," Kiani said. She wiped the tears from her eyes.

I held her closely and tried not to cry for the second time around her. I was a bit confused as to why I couldn't fight the tears, but I realized it's all a part of becoming a man. *Damn, men do cry.* Maybe I was crying because I realized that I was in love . . . so in love I'd do something so stupid for it. Or maybe it was because I was trying so hard to live right, but everything around me was telling me to go left. I knew it was a journey, but I didn't know it was this hard. With the people I had grown close to falling victim to the streets, I was constantly reminded of my old lifestyle. Calvin, Moseley, even Kiani. Perhaps I was crying because I finally realized I could win this battle with myself. No more trying to change—I had changed.

Or it could've just been a mix of everything.

Yeah . . . that's what it was. A mix of everything.

Chapter Thirty-eight

New Life

"AUGH!" Dior yelled out a scream that made the drum of my ear rattle.

It woke the whole house. Moseley and I ran to the room where she was in bed with Calvin having what looked like a nervous breakdown. But it was far from that.

"My contractions are getting worse!" she said, scanning the room. "Oh my Lord! It's time to go to the hospital."

Calvin looked sick. "My woman is about to have my baby," he said. "This can't be happening."

But it was happening. Moseley scrambled through his room for the keys to the car. Meanwhile Calvin began to get ready for the birth of his daughter. Dior waddled her way to the bathroom to fix her hair and put on light makeup. Calvin was hysterical.

"Are you kidding me?" he asked. "Baby, you're putting on makeup for this? Dior!"

"I'm sorry, but I want to have my baby looking fierce," Dior said through the pain. "You know we'll be looking at these pictures years from now."

I smiled at Dior's actions. I wanted my girl to experience
this with me so I called her and told her to meet us at
Cedar Sinai Hospital, where Dior would be giving birth to
a baby girl.

Within forty-five minutes, we were all at the hospital. We
could remain in the delivery room with Dior and Calvin
until it was actually time for her to push. He held her hand
throughout the contractions.

"Hey, mama," Kiani cooed. "How are you feeling?"

Dior, who looked weak and worn, answered, "Oh, I feel
horrible. These contractions are going to be the death of
me. I just want this to be over."

"Poor baby," Kiani said. "I just can't wait to see the
baby."

"Yeah, me too. I promise I'll push as hard as I can." Dior
smiled throughout all her internal pain. She felt a contraction coming on. She grabbed Calvin's hand so tight that he
screamed.

Moseley, Kiani, and I couldn't help but laugh.

"Damn, blood," Moseley said, looking at Calvin. "It's
actually here."

"I know," Calvin answered, never letting go of Dior's
hand. "I'm glad it's here. I really am."

"Well, it needs to hurry and pass," Dior complained. She
asked for the nurse. When the nurse came in, she asked,
"Um, can I have another epidural shot?"

The nurse laughed. "Let me check you out," she answered. She took a peek under the towel covering Dior's
legs and looked at the monitor. "Well, your contractions
are coming along very well. You're about seven centimeters. Once you're nine to ten centimeters dilated, we can
take it from there."

Moseley almost fainted when hearing nine to ten centimeters. "You're kidding, right?" he asked the nurse.

"No, Moseley, the vagina stretches when having a baby.

And you know what? It hurts like all hell," Dior answered, putting on a sarcastic smile.

"I got to get the hell out of here," Moseley said, leaving the delivery room.

Dior and Calvin periodically looked at the contraction monitor and their watches, both patiently awaiting the birth of their daughter.

"Don't y'all look happy," I noticed.

"I'm just ready to have this baby," Dior said. "Any day now!" She spoke up so the nurse could hear her. "I came in here five centimeters. This baby girl needs to speed this process up, damn it!"

"You all ready to be parents?" I asked the happy couple.

They both looked at each other, and couldn't decide on an answer.

"All right, I'll let you off the hook," I said.

Dior let out a blood curdling scream. "This epidural shot is doing nothing for me, and I feel a lot of pressure. I think it's time! Nurse!"

The nurse hurried in and looked at the screen on the monitor. She checked between Dior's legs and saw that she had dilated to nine centimeters.

"Okay, wow! That was quick. You're one of the lucky ones," she said. She paged the doctor and the team of neonatal nurses. They entered into the delivery room as I returned to the waiting room with Moseley and Kiani.

The next announcement we heard was from Calvin, announcing that the baby girl had arrived with the weight of 8 pounds, 5 ounces, and a length of 16 inches.

"And I got to cut the umbilical cord!" said an ecstatic Calvin.

The next time I saw Calvin and Dior together, they were in awe of their daughter. Calvin and Dior kissed, and focused their attention back on their new baby girl. The two couldn't feel any more in love than at this moment.

Epilogue

Two days after the birth of their daughter, Calvin and Dior returned home. Kiani, Moseley, and I spent the next days with the new parents at the house enjoying the sight of the baby girl.

New baby Chanel (how convenient for the designer couple) is perfect in every way. Her full, thick black hair covers her perfectly shaped head. Her piercing brown eyes complement her button nose and pink lips. She is the quintessence of beauty. I wish her all the love, joy and blessings she can handle. Dior asked Shay and me to be the godparents of baby Chanel. I now feel I have a new reason to stick around, to watch my goddaughter grow into something beautiful.

Calvin and Dior cuddle for what seems like the first time in a long time. They each see themselves in baby Chanel. They argue over who she favors more. Calvin got the load of court of his shoulder when he was found innocent of robbery. His lawyers were able to prove he had no prior knowledge about the robbery. With Evan to back up their story in exchange for a shorter sentence, Calvin was a free man.

I'm happy for him. A guy like Calvin deserves to start over. Hopefully he learned from Evan and Mase's mistake. He can dedicate his time to being a father and he'll have baby Chanel to keep him occupied.

Dior has fallen in love with Calvin all over again. Through baby Chanel, she has healed the wounds in their relationship. Calvin allows her to talk to Kevin . . . once a week. It's crazy how she actually obeys that rule. Dior plans to go back to school in the fall, but her main goal is to be the best mother she can be.

Moseley still wants to be a thug, but maybe he'll be put in jail once or twice and quit. Only time will tell . . . and that's the sad part.

Anthony is living his dream, working for Antonia Capponi. He tells us to look out for his clothing on her line this winter. I'm excited for him.

Shay and I still have a broken friendship, and maybe it is better that way. If being cool with Shay requires disrespecting Kiani, I'm not for it. I'll be damned if I ruin things with my girl.

Kiani and I have a healthy and fresh relationship. We took our relationship to the next level and I finally moved into her apartment. She is truly my angel, my everything. Moseley and his boys like to pick on me because I get so lovey-dovey and emotional when it comes to her. From what they say, guys shouldn't be that way. But that's what love does: It puts you out of your element.

I'm making all efforts to live life the right way and I'm inheriting all the positives that come with it. I for damn sure ain't afraid of no cops, the money I make is legit, and I look forward to my next day. It beats living the street life.

I have a good job, built a victorious relationship, and I've been blessed beyond my imagination.

There's the saying that things happen for a reason.

I've been a gangbanger for a reason . . . to become a survivor.

I've been to jail for a reason . . . to learn how to appreciate the gift of life.

I've lost friends for a reason . . . to make room for true ones.

I survived the mean streets of LA . . . a city where our young men are dropping like flies.

I swung at the curveball life threw me, and I knocked it out the park.

Damn, I am immortal.